ZERO TO HERO

BY

KATHRYN R. BIEL

Zero to Hero

DEDICATION

For Michelle:
I could just say you asked if I wanted to talk it out
and leave it at that. But you know I'm an oversharer
and I'll have to mention that I was naked when it
happened.

If you hadn't asked, this book wouldn't have
happened.

AUTHOR'S NOTE

Dear Readers:

While the clinic Andi and Brandon attended on behalf of JustSibs was fictional, JustSibs is not. It is run by Ryan's Case for Smiles, which is a non-profit organization that donates whimsical pillowcases to children in the hospital to remind them they are not defined by their illnesses. Recognizing the all-encompassing trauma that childhood illness takes on the whole family, JustSibs helps siblings navigate life, especially the teen years, while dealing with a chronically ill sibling. You can learn more about them and donate here: https://copingspace.org/siblings/

 Kathryn

Content Warnings: This is a fade to black romance that contains off-the-page consensual encounters. There is discussion of sexual relationships and language around that. Cursing and profanity are present.

Trigger Warnings: parental death, terminal illness, addiction, drunk driving

CHAPTER 1: ANDI

Every interaction with my ex-husband is an opportunity to practice my poker face. Two years of marriage plus four years of divorce is a lot of time to hone this skill, not to mention the 32 years that came before that. It doesn't matter that we're on the phone and he can't see my reaction. I stop packing my suitcase and turn to the mirror to verify my eyelid is not twitching.

Still as stone.

My blue eyes stare back. Not a single dirty blonde hair on my head moves.

Perfect.

"Andi, are you sure you want to do this? You can always back out. I'm sure Nathan will understand."

I'm tempted to blink in an attempt to decipher his true message, but I don't even let myself have that tell. I know what he's saying.

Quit.

Back out.

Back down.

It's like he doesn't know me at all.

That would probably explain why he's my *ex-*husband. FYI, they don't let you list blind ignorance and weaponized incompetence as reasons for divorce, at least not in Massachusetts.

But they totally should.

Lucky for me I got to list adultery. But that's not the point.

After all this time, Mike should know the best way to get me to do something is to tell me I can't. I mean, he was the one who said, "It's not like you're ever going to leave me."

Some people are just slow learners, I guess.

Because, while I may seem passive and quiet, that's only on the exterior. I will die before I back down, especially when it's important.

Like now.

I've worked the last 15 years to get to this point. No way in hell I'm letting this slip through my fingers. I don't care what a logistical nightmare it's created for me. I don't care that it's the worst-case scenario. I don't care that Mike thinks I should back out.

But I do want to know *why* Mike thinks I should.

"That's an interesting option. Why should I consider it?" He's likely to explain more when he thinks I'm actually looking for his advice. This is yet another time when I wish I didn't work with my ex so I could leave him in the past like most people do when they divorce.

"Oh, you know what these two teams can be like."

I don't even need to look at the text from our manager, Nathan Forget, to know what game I've been asked to officiate.

Boston Buzzards vs. Baltimore Terrors.

It's the big time.

The big time.

I've been dreaming about this day for years.

That's right, an official USSL game. To be more specific, the MUSSL. *Men's United States Soccer League*. Not to be confused with the WUSSL, which is the Women's version of the league.

Except, as is true in our society, men are the default, so when people refer to the USSL, they're generally talking about the men's teams. But they always make sure to call the female side the WUSSL, probably because of the resemblance to the word wuss.

Chauvinists.

Obviously, there were no women on the planning board when acronyms were being discussed. Hell, I don't think there are any women on the board even now.

Anyway, I've been a ref for the WUSSL for the past seven years, with over 70 games under my belt with me as the head official, and at least double that me working as other staff. I've been an alternate and an assistant in numerous men's games. This is the first time I will be the head ref in a men's game. In fact, this is the first time for any regular season play in the MUSSL that a woman will be in charge.

To quote Lizzo, *it's about damn time*.

About 15 years ago it looked as if the MUSSL was changing its boys' club ways when Tara Roberts officiated an exhibition match. It was a one-and-done though, and no female has been the head ref since. I don't know if something happened, or if the board thought it was enough to check a box so the womenfolk were happy.

I've earned my spot. No box-checking for me. I've passed all the fitness tests, reporting to the training facility in Atlanta three times a year to participate in the three-day camps where they put us through our paces. My outcomes aren't based on my gender. I'm as fast with just as much endurance and fitness as my male counterparts.

My ex-husband, whom I met at one of those camps by the way, likes to overlook this. It irritates him that we're still competing for the same jobs. That I didn't go away after our divorce.

"Yeah, well, I've got to get my feet wet sometime. At least you'll be there to back me up as my assistant."

Okay, I probably didn't need to needle him that way, but it was a softball lobbed in my direction. This time, I let my mouth slide into a smirk. He can't see it anyway, and it's not like he's ever been adept at reading my tone of voice.

"Do you know why Nate asked you?"

Okay, maybe he did get the jab. Or maybe not. I could read this in a multitude of ways. Is Mike asking why he didn't get promoted to head ref and slide me in as assistant? Is he asking why there is an opening to begin with?

I do know why there's a last-minute vacancy. A large portion of the male staff of the USSLRA—United States Soccer League Referee Association—is heading over to Paris for the Global Games. This is the last regular season game before the world tournament starts in three days. Calvin Memment, who was scheduled for this game, decided to fly to Paris a few days early to get some sightseeing in before the chaos of the games starts. There are no men's games scheduled for the rest of July.

It left an opening, and Nathan thought I'd be the best candidate to fill it. I'm sure that's not what Mike wants to hear. Considering we have to work together tomorrow, I simply respond, "I don't know."

It's better to pretend to be ignorant than to have to deal with his fragile bruised ego. Speaking up for myself has never yielded positive results.

Even as I talk to Mike, I'm wading through the logistical nightmare of changing flights and booking new ones, as well as finding hotels and transportation on short notice. Though I live right outside of Boston, I just did a Wednesday night game in Louisville, Kentucky, which is where I am currently. Now I've got to hightail it to Baltimore for a Saturday noon game instead of going home. I had planned to get a fair amount of work done today for my day job, not to mention my workouts. It'll be challenging with the travel and game prep. It means a few long days so I can meet my work deadlines as well as referee. But there's no way in hell I'm turning down this opportunity.

My celebratory happy dance was not only cut short by the phone call from my ex-husband but also by processing the teams I'll be officiating. I have worked games with both of these teams, and I hate them both equally. The Terrors play super dirty. It wouldn't surprise me if there is mass corruption within the organization. The head coach, Ted Masters, is a douche, but he's a walk in the park as compared to Baltimore Terrors owner Vinny Camacho. Vinny's like a character from a mob movie, complete with greasy hair and pinky rings.

And then there are the Boston Buzzards.

Overall, they aren't a bad team to officiate for.

With the exception of Brandon Nix.

His reputation precedes him in the league. He's amassed enough penalty cards to wallpaper a room. While the majority of his game expulsions are due to getting two yellow cards in one game rather than committing a major offense to draw a red card, he's still missed three games so far this season due to expulsion. Considering we're only about halfway through the 40-game season, that's a high percentage.

He really needs to learn how to check himself before he wrecks himself.

Long story short, any game with him is bound to be difficult. He's sure to challenge call after call, and then his legions of fans, "Nixens," can get equally as rambunctious and raucous.

Let's put it this way, if my car is going to get egged or keyed after a game in retribution, I'd bet the fan was wearing a jersey with Brandon Nix's name and number on it.

It doesn't matter though. It'll be worth it.

I, Andrea Lynn Nichols, will be the very first woman to officiate a regular season MUSSL match. I'll be in the history books. I'll prove that I'm just as good, if not better than a male ref. And despite what some may say, not having a penis will not impact my ability to call a good, fair soccer game.

Hate is a very strong word. Sure, I've used it in the past, but I'm not sure I've actually meant it. I hate the cold. I hate it when people are late. I hate raisins, especially when they are masquerading in cookies as chocolate chips.

Okay, the last one might be true.

But until this very moment, I've never truly understood the depths and visceral power of hate. For the first time in my 38 years of life, I can honestly say I understand what hate is.

Because I hate this man standing in front of me. I hate Brandon Nix.

I hold my ground, my feet firmly planted shoulder-width apart. My arm, ramrod straight, holds the red plastic rectangle in the air for the entire stadium to see. The roar of the crowd is deafening, but I barely process it. I'm trying to keep my chin held high and my gaze unwavering. It's difficult with Brandon Nix mere inches from my face, screaming at me. He's been on this tirade for a solid two minutes. The things he's saying are not exactly kind.

His brown eyes blaze, his sweat-drenched hair bobs in a stupid man bun on the top of his head. I can feel his hot breath and spit dance across my face. It takes everything I have not to wipe it off in disgust. He's practically pounding his chest like the ape he is.

"Are you blind? He's been up my fucking ass all game."

My poker face doesn't move. My hand stays high in the air.

Brandon Nix keeps yelling, now his hands go to his hips. I've watched enough nature documentaries to know this is typical male posturing to make him seem bigger. We're practically nose to nose.

Objects in mirror are closer than they appear.

I just need him to take a step—or ten—back.

Though I want to knee him in the 'nads, I don't move a muscle. I'm not lowering my hand until he stops screaming in my face.

The goalie, CC Campbell, finally pulls Brandon back. I continue on with standard procedure, documenting the player's name, foul, and time of foul. I repeat the information into my headset and am ready to move on with game play.

Without Brandon Nix.

It's not my fault this is his second yellow card during the game. In soccer, yellow cards are cautions for offenses that are larger than a minor foul but not serious. When a player receives two yellow cards, it equates to a red. Soccer math. I didn't make the rules; I strictly enforce them.

Red cards are used for serious misconduct and discipline. For egregious offenses, they may result in suspension over multiple games. At a minimum, the player cannot start the next game. And the most damaging impact is the player is not replaced with a substitute for the remainder of this one, leaving his teammates shorthanded. It can be a long second half when a player gets sent off early in the game.

Brandon Nix should have considered that before he kicked Trevyon Wallis-Smalls while they were both attempting to play the ball. Hell, that kick would have been a red card all on its own.

I feel a hand on my shoulder. I immediately shrug, jerking it off. It's also a high offense to touch a referee. I turn, ready to issue another red card only to see Mike.

He puts his hand over his mic and leans in. "Are you okay? Do you need to leave? I can step in."

I forget my stoic face for a moment as my brows raise in surprise. "What? Why? No."

I turn around, shaking my head, and position the ball for the indirect penalty kick that will start the game back up.

I cannot believe my ex-husband thinks a blowhard like Brandon Nix is enough to shake me. I may hate the way he plays soccer, and I hate the way he conducts himself as a player even more. But to step down simply because Brandon Nix got in my face and questioned my call?

That's ridiculous.

CHAPTER 2: BRANDON

This ref doesn't know what she's doing. I can't believe she gave me my second yellow and had me sent off.

Okay, I did totally kick him, but he deserved it. Trevyon has been throwing jabs and pushing me all match. That's not what put me over the edge though.

He deserved a spike to the nuts for what he said.

If only I hadn't already drawn a yellow card, I'd still be in the game.

That first yellow was a bullshit call. It wasn't a handball at all.

Okay, maybe a little, but the refs never call something that barely grazes the outside of the arm as it goes by. Leave it to the lady ref. That's really why I got in her face. She shouldn't have called it.

Now, here I am, sitting in the locker room, thumb up my ass, with nothing to do. I won't get to start the next game either. It sucks enough that there's a month break before the next match due to the Global Games, and now it'll be even longer for me.

I want to punch something—or someone—but I don't want to end up with a broken hand. Again.

I make a colossal mistake by pulling out my phone.

Dad: Way to go. How many reds this season?

If there's one thing I can't do, it's ignore a text from my dad.

Me: 4

His reply is immediate.

Dad: I don't know why they keep you on the team.

Thanks, Dad.

I mean, I ask myself that all the time. It wouldn't shock me at all to get called into Coach Janssen's office as soon as we get back to Boston.

I don't expect to get called over at halftime. In the past when I've been set off, staff simply ignored me.

Yeah, it's totally better that way.

"Do I even need to ask?" Coach Janssen tents his fingers under his chin.

"It wasn't a handball in the first place."

"Technically, it was. I watched the replay."

I cock my head. "Oh, come on. You know that shouldn't have been called."

Coach raises an eyebrow slightly. "That's up for debate. But that's not what I'm talking about."

"He was up my ass all half. Shoving, throwing elbows. He stepped on me at least once. So I gave it back." I don't bother mentioning the comments muttered under Trevyon Wallis-Smalls's breath throughout the opening minutes of the game. Bringing that up and letting Coach know I reacted to it is not going to help my cause. Nobody cares about my sob story, so I'm not going to mention it.

"That's not what I'm talking about either."

I shrug, clueless. Sure, I threw my shirt when I got off the field and stomped off like a petulant child, but what else did he expect me to do? It's bullshit. And it's not like I'm the only one who does something like that.

"I'm talking about Andi Nichols."

That name means nothing to me. "Who's Andy Nichols?" All I can think of is the kid from *Toy Story*, but that would be weird for Coach to bring up now. "I don't know him."

"No, but you know *her*. She's the head ref for the game."

Oh.

"She made a bad call, and I let her know."

Coach sits back, folding his arms over his chest. "Are you a member of USSLRA?"

I shake my head, shifting from one foot to the other, trying to ignore the pit growing in my stomach.

Coach continues. "Have you been trained by USSLRA?"

"Obviously not, since I'm a player and not a ref." My mouth doesn't know when to quit. It should, but it has a mind of its own.

"Then stop thinking you have jurisdiction over the pitch and shut your damn mouth."

Bjorn Janssen is one of the most laid-back people I've ever met, and he rarely cusses. Oh fuck. He's going to fire me right here and now. I have to do something. I say the first thing that pops into my head. Naturally. "I am your leading scorer."

"But you can't score when you're suspended. You need to get your act together, or you won't have a place here."

I can only imagine what my ever-supportive dad would have to say about me getting fired for my mouth. For once, I stay quiet. Instead, I purse my lips together and nod.

"I don't want to let you go, Brandon, but you're backing me into a corner. Bob Miller doesn't like paying you to sit on the bench because you can't control your mouth."

"I speak the truth as I see it."

Coach scrubs his hand over his face. "That's what I'm talking about. You need to focus a little less on speaking your truth and a little more on thinking about your public image. No more screwups. You're good, but nobody's irreplaceable. Consider yourself on probation for the rest of the season."

His words hit like spikes to the shin.

Without shin guards.

Coach stands and walks around me, leaving me all alone in the tiny office of the guest locker room. I don't move until the locker room is empty. It's not like I can go back out on the field, even to watch from the bench.

I want to take a long, hot shower, but these locker rooms are utter crap. They're small and dirty and painted the brightest shade of pink this side of a bottle of Pepto Bismol. You'd think teams would want to show off their state-of-the-art facilities to their guests, but not the Baltimore Terrors.

Oh no, they want their opponents to be as uncomfortable as possible. They also want to use a little psychological warfare too, by insinuating the opposing team are girls.

Dumb asses.

I could wait for the team and take the bus back to the hotel, but considering we have a month's break starting when this game ends, I might just start my vacation early. My teammates certainly won't miss me, especially since I left them shorthanded.

I order an Uber and leave the stadium mid-game. No one's even going to notice I'm gone.

CHAPTER 3: ANDI

My alarm sounds, waking me for my flight home from Baltimore to Boston at way too early of an hour. I was so keyed up after the game last night that I could barely sleep, let alone analyze the day. Even with the lack of rest, I am still on cloud nine.

I am officially part of history.

Someday, sometime in the distant future, some inebriated dude will feel like a million bucks because he supplies my name during a heated round of trivia at a pub.

I will forever be seen and remembered.

That's not the reason why I wanted to officiate a MUSSSL game. I was just doing a job that I loved. And then, I saw I had more room to grow, so I grew. It's just gravy that I got to shatter a glass ceiling in the process.

I might even get to quit my day job.

Now that—*that*—would be a true victory.

Only the most successful and upper-tier referees get to do this full-time. Me, I'm working for a health insurance company, reviewing letters of medical necessity and either approving or denying coverage whenever I'm not on the pitch.

I actually went to school for physical therapy, but it's hard to have a practice when you have a second job that requires lots of travel. Plus, it wasn't a job I loved. My parents thought it would be a good fit for me, and not knowing what else to do, I became a physical therapist. That is until I started traveling so much for soccer.

So, I went to work for the enemy because I can read letters and write judgments anywhere.

My day job is the antithesis of everything I wanted to do in life. But maybe, just maybe, things will change now.

And also, maybe, since the game was a success with no incidents or controversy, the MUSSL will employ me more frequently in the head position. The salary rate is higher for MUSSL games than for WUSSL games.

Don't even get me started on that.

Maybe it's hazard pay for dealing with all those uber inflated egos.

I get that the MUSSL has better viewership and better sponsors, but it's not like the game is less work. It's the same amount of time. The same amount of running. It's the same amount of physical training. The same amount of prep work. Just for less money because it's women's sports.

But with the higher salary rate the men's games pay and more games, I might be able to swing this as my only job. Maybe.

It's a lot of maybes to base my life on.

It'd be nice though. I've burnt my candle at both ends for so long, I'm not sure I even have a wick left.

I definitely don't have time for dating or a social life or anything fun. The expression "I am the job" was meant for me.

Once I'm through security at the airport, I have a few minutes to think, but I'm interrupted as my phone dings with a text alert.

Benj: Not too many boos.

Of course, my brother would lead with that. There were only a few when I emerged from the tunnel, game ball in hand, to perform the coin toss at midfield to start the game.

Me: I expected more.

Sad to say, but I totally did. There's a reason there haven't been female referees in the MUSSL. Good ole misogyny at its finest. This sport, and this league especially, don't think women are equal to men.

Me: Mike tried to talk me out of doing it.

Benjamin is not a fan of my ex-husband. On more than one occasion, he's offered to "accidentally" run Mike over with his power wheelchair. One of these days, I may take him up on it.

Benj: That made it better, him running the lines.

Considering the closest to a traditional wife I'm ever going to be is a Petty Crocker, I totally agree with my brother. It was great to be the official with Mike being the assistant ref.

    Me: Pretty spotless game, I'd say.

    Benj: Ehh, not quite.

My brother's body might not cooperate most days, but his eyes and brain are sharp. What did he see that I didn't? His favorite hobby is to tell me about my missed calls.

    Me: What'd I miss?

I start to worry. It's hard enough officiating a game. It's doubly so as a woman. I know my performance will be under heavy scrutiny. It's another one of those double standards. Sure, male refs will get put on notice for bad calls, but the tolerance of judgment narrows considerably when one has a vagina and breasts.

Our professional league, the United States Soccer League Referee Association, has an entire staff that watches our games and judges our performances. We're scored on our calls, receiving points for correct calls and losing points for incorrect calls and missed calls. They have the benefit of watching recordings and replays, while we have to make snap decisions on the spot with only one point of view. The USSL and the USSLRA are looking to keep up with the British Football League by introducing video replay next season. Until then, we have to try to improve our skills based on this points system.

    Me: How many points?

    Benj: No points. The whole thing with Nix.

Pfft.

Me: That's not a thing. That's him in practically every game. He's a blowhard. I don't know why the Buzzards keep his contract.

Benj: Because he's their best scorer. But that's not what I'm talking about.

Me: ???

Benj: I hope I'm wrong, but you know I never am

Brat, he's right about barely being wrong.

I shrug as if he were here to see me. The thing about Nix is a non-issue. If it didn't cost me points, then I don't care. The more points I have, the more likely I am to get primary referee jobs and to be able to move up to a Level 2.

Me: It is what it is. I called what I saw. If he doesn't want to be ejected from games, he should play clean. That's on him, not on me.

I might sound confident in my texts, but I'm sure Benj can see through it. I spend the entire flight home, as well as the next day and a half, obsessively watching the game tape just to review my calls. If I'm not working, I'm looking at every minute of play. I don't even turn the TV on.

Finally satisfied, I text my brother again.

Me: My game was clean. I can't find any point deductions.

Benj: Have you been reviewing it this entire time?

My brother knows me well. He's about the only person who sees me this clearly. Ironic, considering I haven't seen him in person in almost a year. The pang of missing him hits me hard in the chest.

Me: I had to do some actual work and travel back home. But yes, for the most part.

My mind whirring, I open my work calendar and see many more white spots than normal for this time of the year. With the Global Games in Paris right now, there's a month-long hiatus in seasonal play for the MUSSL.

The WUSSL still has games, but considering I've been working both leagues for the past few seasons, it's enough to give me some spare time I'm not used to having.

Of course, it means the men will play into December this year, instead of wrapping up in November like normal. Looks like no winter holidays in the Keys like in the past.

Maybe I should look at going to visit my brother in Colorado, though December is always a risky time to try to travel there.

Hell, I should visit him now.

I have eleven days before my next game in Birmingham. That's plenty of time.

I'm looking up flights when Mike calls. Why can't he just text like everyone else? Or better yet, why can't he just leave me alone?

"What are you up to?"

"Trying to book a flight to Colorado Springs."

"What's out there? There aren't any games there this week, are there?"

He's so worried about me getting ahead that he doesn't even consider the Global Games hiatus. "No, I'm going to see Benj."

"Benj?"

"Yeah, my brother. Benjamin. You know, he was my person of honor in our wedding."

"Right. I forgot."

I'll bet he forgot. He forgot a lot when we were married, like he wasn't supposed to be sleeping with anyone else. Whatever. It's in the past, and I really don't care about him enough to let it bother me. I click a few more options. "Damn, flights are expensive. It's hard to swallow this price knowing I'm not getting reimbursed from the league for it."

"Yeah, but the $900 from the game this weekend should help, right?"

I hadn't considered that. I quickly open my banking app to make sure the money has been deposited before I purchase my airline tickets.

Except the new deposit is for $678.96, after taxes.

This doesn't make sense. "How much did you say it is for a game? I usually get $650 for a WUSSL game." A men's game should be much higher.

"Not for the assistant. For the ref." Mike was always good at mansplaining. I know what I get paid, down to the penny.

"I'm not talking about the assistant. What do you get paid as a Level 3 ref per game?"

"We get $900 for reffing, $420 as the assistant, and $300 for the backup assistant."

I open up my USSLRA employee portal so I can look at my paystubs a little closer because his numbers don't make sense. I got paid $738 for the Buzzards–Terrors game. That's not an error. I say as much to Mike.

He's uncharacteristically quiet.

The one time I want him to tell me what's going on, he doesn't say a blessed thing.

"What? Why aren't you talking? What's going on? Mike, are you still there?" Maybe we disconnected. It would be the only logical explanation.

He lets out a deep sigh. "Andi, you're not going to like it."

"What?" I'm on my feet now, pacing around my small apartment.

"What are your rates for ladies' games?"

"My rates are $650, $305 for assistant, and $217 for backup."

Another sigh. I swear he's stalling to piss me off. Even though I wish I could reach through the phone and pull the answer out of him physically. Instead, I wait, not moving and not making any noise.

I'm fairly confident my ex would describe me as infinitely patient. He has no idea I'm practically crawling out of my skin right now.

"I make $793, $372, and $265 for ladies' games. Don't make this weird. You don't want to do anything that could jeopardize your career."

My mind is working overtime trying to process what he's saying. We were in the same orientation group with the United States Soccer League Referee Association, so we have the same level of experience. We're both considered Level 3s, and we have about the same number of games under our belts, give or take a few. I think I may have more than Mike at this time. I don't tend to request time off for things like fishing trips with my buddies. The numbers he's reporting to me make no sense.

Unless …

There's only one reason for this.

Also, I hate that he refers to them as "ladies' games" instead of "women's." I can't tell if he's being passive-aggressive or ignorant. It doesn't really matter about the intent. The effect is the same.

I make Mike repeat his numbers so I can write them down and then make up some bullshit excuse so I can end the phone call. And then I crunch the numbers.

No matter how many times I look at it, the same answer is apparent. Mike gets paid more than I do because I'm female and he's male. Eighteen percent more. Not to mention the pay is higher for men's games than women's.

I know it shouldn't surprise me, but it does. Rage runs through my veins hot and fast. In the solitude of my apartment, I let my poker face slip. I don't feel like being the bigger person. I don't want to be the picture of stoicism. It's hard enough being a woman. It's doubly so in an industry that is so openly sexist. In an uncharacteristic move, I open ClikClak, determined to take my outrage to social media.

However, the first post I see is enough to feel like I've been doused with an entire vat of ice-cold water.

CHAPTER 4: ANDI

If I had to make a list of things I'd want to see blasting all over social media regarding the world of soccer, they would be, in no particular order: coverage about the first female to referee a regulation league MUSSL game, coverage about the wage gap between male and female referees in sports, coverage about the wage—and salary—gap for women's sports as compared to their male counterparts, and coverage from the Global Games, since I can't afford to go.

The *very* last thing I want to see is video footage of Brandon "Bad Breath" Nix screaming in my face.

Over and over and over.

For the record, no one else calls him by that nickname, but I doubt anyone else has been that close recently. Seriously, if you're going to get in people's faces like that, at least eat a mint beforehand.

If that weren't bad enough, the comments. *The comments*.

Female referees should stay in female football.

Why are there even female referees? This is a man's sport.

She should stick to the kitchen.

She should just go be a commentator where her opinion won't hurt the game.

It's giving offside, I think?

He looks like he wants to kiss her.

The last comment makes me want to vomit. Or at least laugh hysterically. Brandon Nix and me? It's a whole lot of nope.

To be sure, there are a lot of great videos of me, with inspirational songs, standing up to Nix. That's great. I want to be a role model to young women everywhere. That's a bonus with being a trailblazer.

But much more of the focus is about Brandon and me.

Which is not the issue.

It shouldn't be the issue.

Yet because of this blowhard, that's all anyone is focusing on.

And then, I check my email.

Andrea,

Please schedule a time to meet on Zoom to discuss this weekend's match. The sooner, the better. Sydney will send you the link.

Regards, Nate

The air whooshes out of me like I've been punched in the gut.

This is certainly nothing to laugh about.

I'm going to lose it all before I even start. All because of Brandon Nix. It's official. He's definitely worse than raisins in cookies masquerading as chocolate chips.

I pace around my apartment, gesticulating with my arms and arguing with the air, pleading my case. Except there's no one to hear me and no one to sympathize. I can talk to Benj about it when I get to Colorado, but since he doesn't know I'm coming yet, I don't want to call and ruin his surprise.

And I know if I get on the phone with him now, I'll undoubtedly say something. I'm too heated not to rant, and I know I'd spoil the surprise. It's better if I don't make contact until I can pull my emotions together.

No one needs to hear me complain.

It's not like I'm going to go to Mike with this.

Since I work remotely, I no longer have a work bestie either.

I'm totally alone.

I don't know why I didn't realize it before.

Maybe because I was always so busy traveling here and there, running to stadiums, and trying to cram my day job in, or maybe because I spent a lifetime making myself invisible, I never took the time to realize that I don't have any close human connections anymore.

It was easy when Mike and I were married because we had each other. We socialized mostly with other male refs. Obviously, I'm not calling any of them up to commiserate.

Knowing I won't be able to rest until I get this settled, I email Sydney, Nathan's assistant. Waiting to hear back from her is pure agony. Lucky for me, it's only about 20 minutes of pure agony. Nathan's available now.

This is so not good.

I don't know why. Even Benj said my calls were okay.

Maybe I'm getting a promotion?

My gut doesn't say so.

Maybe Nathan's discovered that it was a clerical error in my paycheck and not a system-wide policy of discrimination and sexism.

Even the most optimistic person wouldn't buy that one.

I'm at a loss.

"Thank you for responding so quickly," Nathan starts, not wasting any time the minute I join the Zoom.

"Of course." I nod slightly, the only movement in my still posture.

"I won't beat around the bush," Nathan says.

"I appreciate that."

"The USSLRA has some concerns regarding the game you officiated this past week."

I swallow hard, clenching my jaw, waiting for him to continue.

"There has been a fair amount of coverage on social media, and it's not favorable."

"I'm not sure what you mean." He's giving me no context clues.

"The incident with Brandon Nix."

Oh, that. "I'm not the first official to send off Brandon Nix, and I can guarantee I will not be the last."

Nathan pauses on the screen. For a moment, I think there's a glitch in the connection and he's frozen. But then I notice the pendulum of his wall clock moving back and forth. Back and forth. It's not an internet issue, it's him.

Damn, I could learn a lot about maintaining my poker face from this man.

Finally, he speaks. "Brandon Nix has quite the reputation on and off the field."

I don't often follow the personal lives of soccer players, unless it blows up huge, like with Xavier Henry and that Ophelia girl from ClikClak. "My only concern is with how a player conducts his- or herself during the game, on the field. The rest is none of my business. I don't want to enter a game with preconceived notions that will affect my ability to call a proper game."

At last, Nathan raises his eyebrows a fraction. If I hadn't been staring so intently at my screen, I might not have noticed.

My nerves fray the last tiny bit of my patience. "Please just spit it out. I obviously have no idea what you're referring to."

"After analysis of the altercation with Brandon Nix, there are quite a few people who are speculating that there is some sort of romantic involvement between you and Mr. Nix."

My internal self breaks out into a side-splitting guffaw, laughing so hard that my entire body convulses, and tears roll down my cheeks. My external self raises one eyebrow a millimeter and the corner of my mouth quirks with incredulity.

Apparently, that was too much emotion to show. Dammit. A quick glance at the screen shows that my boss does not appreciate my response.

"I'm glad you find this amusing, but we must take this seriously. It could have grave consequences. If you need to be refreshed, I'd advise you to review Policy 3.4-7 in our conduct manual which prohibits fraternization with players."

Fraternization? Nathan is not kidding. I steel my expression. I've got my game face on. "Right. Of course."

"This game garnered extra attention and coverage due to your role as head referee. There have been many critics who do not think a woman should be officiating in the men's league. That they have no business being together on the field because something might happen with one of the players."

If I were letting any muscles in my face move, it would be the ones that roll my eyes at this antiquated thinking. Of course, if a man and a woman share the same space, there must be some sort of sexual attraction happening. There's no way a woman can exist outside her role as a sexual creature.

Nathan keeps talking, unaware of my distaste for this reductionist, chauvinistic train of thought. "As well as that women cannot keep up with the pace of men, or that they do not know the game as well. Giving even the slightest hint of impropriety only adds fuel to that fire. Samuel Fredericks has given the directive to expand our DEI, which is how your name got brought up to fill Calvin's vacancy."

This revelation feels like a punch to the gut. I thought I was given the job because I was the best suited for it. As a USSLRA referee, I participate in and am graded on my physical fitness three times per year. Like every other referee, my games are reviewed and scored. My tallies on both the physical achievements as well as the game scores are solidly average for a Level 3 ref.

Not a Level 3 female ref, but of all referees.

I'd thought the patriarchal views that held the USSLRA in a tight grip were from upper management. I never realized Nathan was part of that.

"If you are to be given this opportunity again, you will need to make sure that you are presented as a professional referee first and foremost, both on and off the field. We do not want to draw attention to your gender at all. It cannot be the focus of the game. And there certainly cannot be any sort of flirtation or smiles or coy looks to players. If you want to be successful with the USSLRA, please do not let something like this tarnish your otherwise stellar record."

I don't have to worry about my reply because I am too stunned to speak. I believe I nod as Nathan ends the call, but then I sit there in silence. His words replay on an endless loop in my head.

Flirtation. Smile. Coy.

There was none of that during the game. Not one single iota. And for Nathan to suggest that there was is way out of line. All because ... what? Why? Oh right. Those stupid comments on ClikClak. I cannot believe that some lowlife bottom feeders on an app could skew reality so completely that now my boss is involved.

Another word he said joins the loop in my brain.

If.

There's no other way to interpret it other than a thinly veiled threat. Or not so thinly veiled. It's like he's looking for a reason for me not to succeed. My career could be over before it starts, all because some jackhole can't control his temper, and I happen to have been born with a uterus. I cannot believe in this day and age we're still thinking like this.

This is complete and utter bullshit.

CHAPTER 5: BRANDON

This is complete and utter bullshit.

My name is being dragged through the mud like I'm some sort of cretin. How I attacked that poor, helpless lady referee like a caveman. That I was seconds away from slinging her over my shoulder and carrying her off to bed.

As if.

I get it. I'm a hothead. I'm a loud-mouth asshole.

At least that's what my father's been telling me for as long as I can remember.

But there's no way in hell I was hitting on a lady ref in the middle of the soccer game.

Especially not that one lady ref. The one who might have cost me my career.

Not to mention, I do just fine with the ladies. They flock to me. I can find a Nixen anywhere. I'm not desperate.

At least not about that. My career is another story.

I'm officially on probation with the Buzzards. One more misstep and I'm toast. Something about violating the Players' Code of Conduct that was in my contract.

I should probably read it over to find out exactly what I can and can't do. To do that, I'd have to call my agent, but I try to talk to him as little as possible.

My advice for up-and-coming athletes: don't let your father be your agent. It seemed smart when Lionel Messi did it, but it hasn't worked out so well for me.

Mostly because we don't get along. Like, can't be in the same room or be civil to each other. In my defense, he started it.

But I can't end it, since he's all I have left. So, I'll do what I always do. I won't think about it. It's easier that way.

My phone dings with a text alert. I'm so relieved it's not my dad—again—that I don't think before I look at it.

Landon: Dude, you're viral

Landon Stubbs is the bane of my existence. He's a thorn in my side. He's a pain in my ass.

But he's a pretty decent midfielder, so I let some of it slide. He's probably my best friend, if I was going to have one of those.

Me: Shut up

Landon: Have you seen all the coverage? You going toe to toe with Andi Nichols. She put you in your place.

Me: You're a douchebag
Landon: Takes one to know one

After those words of encouragement, I do the only responsible thing and fall down the rabbit hole which is the internet.

The handball was still a bullshit call, but she didn't do half bad on the rest of the game. Actually, she was pretty fair. She didn't back down when I got in her face, which says something about her. If only she'd heard what Trevyon said to me, she'd probably have kicked him herself. But no, I'm the bad guy here.

I'm the guy who could get fired over this.

I'm half-tempted to text my sister, but she doesn't need my problems too. Her life is enough of a train wreck without my baggage. Still, it's been a few days since I've heard from her. That has me worried. My problems can wait. What if she's not okay?

Me: Hey Jess, what's up?

Then, I try not to panic when she doesn't answer right away. For some people, it could mean they're busy. They're in the shower. Or at work. Or having sex. Doing something that shouldn't be interrupted.

But when Jessica doesn't answer, I worry that she's on a bender somewhere. Passed out. Maybe overdosing in a restaurant bathroom in the bad part of town. And trust me, wherever she is, it's the bad part of town.

In theory, she's clean right now, but I've heard that line more times over the past dozen years than I can count. Because of that, her relapsing will be my fear every day until the day one of us gets put into the ground. And with her history, it could be any day now. Any phone call could be *the one.*

There's nothing I can do from my house in Walpole, Massachusetts. Jessica, last I knew, was on a ranch in Wyoming or some bullshit like that. Finding herself while communing with nature. I think it was a scam to get cheap labor by billing it as a healing experience to help with recovery. It wouldn't surprise me if it's a cult or something, because that'd be just like my sister to accidentally join a cult.

I don't care. She needs to stay out west. Far away from me and my teammates. To be fair, she hasn't been to see me since I played for the Nevada Renegades and Trevyon Wallis-Smalls was my teammate.

Las Vegas and my sister do not mix. In fact, it was that visit that he was so eloquently referring to as he jabbed an elbow into my side. He's lucky he only got a spike to the shin. I should have bashed his face in for what he said.

Doesn't he know what happens in Vegas is supposed to stay in Vegas?

Of course, none of it was untrue. It was just uncalled for. It's not cool to go after someone's personal life like that. No one talks about my family like that and walks away. Sure, we're the poster children for dysfunction, but that's nobody's business but ours.

And since I'm not allowed to pummel anyone's face in—I'm fairly sure *that's* a violation of my contract—I channel all my rage and frustration and fear the only way I know how.

Working out until I drop.

It only takes me 90 minutes to complete my 10-mile treadmill run. Not nearly long enough to take the edge off my nerves. Another hour or two lifting weights, and I'm finally spent enough for my brain to quiet down.

As I soak in my ice tub post workout, I can only imagine what I'd say if I was ever interviewed in *Sports Illustrated* and they ask about how I stay in such peak physical condition.

Well, you see, my family is super messed up, and I'm afraid I'm going to become an addict like my sister or the biggest prick in the world like my dad, so I work out instead.

I also enjoy other physical forms of working out, if you know what I mean, but that seems like too much effort. I have absolutely zero capacity to deal with a woman's bullshit right now. And trust me, if there's a woman, there will be bullshit.

By the time I'm done with my workout, I'm so physically exhausted I think about passing out rather than walking all the way upstairs to my bedroom. My small A-frame was meant to have a main-floor bedroom, but I converted it into a home gym. My room is now the loft space upstairs.

The house is ugly. The decor is dated and in desperate need of an overhaul. Even so, it feels lived-in and cozy, which hasn't encouraged me to pick up my speed with the renovations. It was also super expensive for the half-acre lot it's on. But it looks out onto a lake. Large sliding glass doors give a view from both levels of the house. That's what makes it all worth it.

Plus, it's secluded and off the beaten path for being in a pretty congested area of the country. I'm not sure any therapist would agree that solitude is my friend, but I think I'm doing just fine.

Except for the whole probation thing.

Speaking of my therapist, I shoot a text to Watson Ross to ask for an appointment, because I don't actually have an outside therapist. Sure, Watson's the team's sports psychologist, but I'm sure I can talk through whatever's bothering me and get it under control so I don't go fully off the rails.

It's not like I have to talk about my childhood or growing up or my sister or anything like that. I mean, I might have to get into my sister, if I'm talking about the game against the Terrors. It'll be fine.

Actually, this will be good. Coach Janssen made our goalie, Callaghan Entay, go talk to Ross last winter when his shoulder was messed up. He got his shit straightened out, and he's now over in Paris repping the US as goalie in the Global Games.

Lucky bastard.

I could have been there.

I was blackballed.

Everyone knows I'm one of the best forwards in the league. But no one wants to give me a chance. They all want their horse to get ahead in the race. I'm no one's horse.

I'm a lone wolf.

Just how I like it.

No one wants to be around me anyway.

And that's fine with me. Just let me play soccer and score goals and leave me alone.

CHAPTER 6: BRANDON

I 'm not sure I'm the right person to help you."

I stare at Watson Ross. I literally just told him that I felt like everyone in my life deserts me, and then he says this. "You're joking, right? You're shitting me. Is this therapy humor or something? Are you gonna tell this to your shrink friends later on when you're at the bar?"

"Brandon, you didn't let me finish. What I was trying to say before you interrupted me was that while I'm not sure I'm the right person to help you, I'd like to give it a try. I might have to consult with colleagues if this goes in directions that are outside my wheelhouse."

I fold my arms over my chest. I'm not so sure about this guy. Coach swears he's a miracle worker, and I've seen my teammates get better after talking to him.

"I'm only here because they put me on probation. You know that, right? All I need you to do is help me not lose my shit on the pitch anymore so I stop getting carded."

"Was attending therapy part of your probation?" Ross asks, pushing his glasses back up on the bridge of his nose. He seriously looks like they called central casting and asked for a "nerdy white guy." I bet he got shoved in a locker or two growing up.

Hell, if I'd gone to school with him, I'd probably have been the one to put him there. And I wonder why I don't have friends.

It's fine. I don't need friends. I don't need anyone.

"No, I thought it might help, though I'm not sure what the problem is really. I have a temper. So what? So do most people. I don't take bullshit from anyone, and I call them out. Most people can't handle that, and they think I'm the problem. It's easier than looking at themselves. And they don't want to be around my kind of honesty, so they leave."

They leave me.

Whatever. I'm better off anyway.

"Well, there's being honest, and there's being rude." Ross sits back in his chair. "They're not the same thing and should not be used interchangeably."

"Rude?" I jump to my feet. "You want to know what's rude? Telling someone in the middle of a game that your sister entertained him and a bunch of friends, except he didn't put it so nicely. Use your imagination. That's fucking rude. He's lucky I didn't deck him. So I spiked him a little. I didn't deserve to be thrown out for that."

It takes me a second to realize what I've said aloud. I sink back down to the couch and look at the ground. I can't believe I told Watson Ross that about Jessica.

I should be protecting her, not spreading gossip.

Of course, I don't doubt Trevyon's story is true. She's a hot mess.

"I'm not condoning violence, but I can see your point. But why did you yell at the referee? I've seen the video."

"The whole world has seen the video," I mumble, sitting back with my arms crossed over my chest. I still can't look up at him.

"It's understandable you were upset about that. It does indeed sound like a very rude thing to say. But were you mad at the referee or at the player who said it?"

"Both." I nod, finally able to look up and meet Ross's eyes. "In all honesty, if I could have pummeled Trevyon Wallis-Smalls to a pulp with my bare hands, I would have. And that ref! Don't get me started on her. The only reason she called the handball in the first place is because she was afraid of messing up and getting flak for it. She never should have called it. Every other ref in the league would have let it slide. Then, my second offense would only have been my first, and I would have been able to play the rest of the game. I shouldn't have to be punished because she was trying to prove herself."

"So, your probation and the possible consequences of another infraction are because of the ref?"

I nod. I do not understand why people have such a hard time going to therapy. This guy understands me totally.

I walk out of Watson Ross's office feeling great. If I'd known it would be like that, I would have gone a lot sooner. My good mood lasts for exactly the ten minutes it takes to drive to the Buzzards training facility.

The moment I exit the car, I'm assaulted by the press. Okay, it's like three people trying to film me, but it doesn't matter. All it takes is one asshole with a cellphone camera, and then the next thing you know, you're viral.

I want to run past them with my coat pulled up over my head, but then it would look like I was ashamed of myself. I'm not. I'm proud of who I am and what I've overcome to get to this point.

I'm one of the best soccer players in the country.

The Boston Buzzards are lucky to have me. I'm certainly part of their complete turnaround in the past two seasons. They should remember that.

I should remind them.

I pull my bag out of the back of my car, trying to ignore the onlookers. Though, truth be told, one doesn't really fly under the radar too much driving a blue metallic Porsche Taycan GTS Sport Turismo. Yes, the name of my car is a mouthful, but it's the flashiest thing my professional soccer career has provided me.

My dad told me I couldn't drive my piece of shit Ford Explorer after I signed my last contract. Considering the average salary is in the $300,000 range, and I'm pulling in almost a mil a year, he didn't think I should be seen driving around in a car that my mom purchased in 2005.

I liked it because it was hers. My soccer stuff was always in the back, and we spent many hours driving to practices and games and tournaments. I had a lot of good memories from that vehicle. Let's face it, with it being a Ford and all, the money spent keeping the damn thing running was almost as much as my new Porsche. But my new Porsche doesn't connect me with her.

I also think that's why my dad pushed me to the new car.

Whatever. Now people know it's me driving around the stadium and practice facilities. Being seen is part of my agent's strategy for keeping me—and him—well paid. If I make a name for myself, the Buzzards are less likely to move on from me.

Until now.

As if he received a cosmic signal that I was thinking about this very thing, my dad texts me.

Dad: Don't forget your contract is up at the end of this season. If you want to keep playing, you need to get yourself in line. Don't fuck this up.

Seriously, my dad-slash-agent should go into business with his motivational sayings, like "Don't fuck this up." Then, maybe he could make his money off of something else besides me.

Hell, I never wanted to even play soccer in the first place. I wanted to play football, but my mom was afraid I'd get hurt, so soccer it was. Turns out I was a star from the first time I set foot on the field.

Prodigy and phenom were words bandied about when I was a kid. It was as if fate took the choice out of my hands and before I knew it, I was a soccer player.

I eventually grew to love it, and soccer's been a constant while the rest of my life went to shit. At least I knew what to expect when I was there. Practicing, training, playing, I knew what was coming. They were never going to hit me like an out-of-control pickup truck and totally upend my life.

Except now. One more wrong move, and it'll all be over. And then what? I didn't go to college. I have no skills off the pitch. When people say soccer is life, they don't know how accurate that is to someone like me.

I should remind the Buzzards how valuable I am, so they don't throw me away like yesterday's coffee cup. As much as I want to run away, I stop and smile for the aspiring paparazzi who are about to ambush me. A few minutes of cheesy mugging might be all it takes to erase that other video from the trending watches on ClikClak.

All I need to do is keep giving them new material so the other thing goes away.

It's as easy as making a penalty kick.

CHAPTER 7: ANDI

I'm fine. No, really, I am.

At least that's what I keep telling myself.

I am the furthest thing from fine that I can get. All because … society sucks, that's why. And because some baboon named Brandon Nix had to get in my face.

That's it.

And now, instead of being upset that the USSLRA pays its women referees less than they pay their men and being able to get fair pay for fair work, I'm put on notice that my career could be over because of a *perceived*—what? I don't even know what to call it. Flirtation? Impropriety? Attraction?

HA! That makes me laugh. Brandon Nix? Foul-tempered, loud-mouthed, hasn't-had-a-haircut-this-decade Brandon Nix? The thought of anything with that man has me cackling away like a maniac. I don't remember the last time I laughed like this. You know, the gut-busting kind where you literally bend in half and slap your knee. Because I'm alone, I let myself laugh until I notice tears falling in drops onto the floor.

This is so unfair.

That's a familiar mantra in my life. Familiar enough to pull me up straight, my face quickly falling back into its neutral resting position.

I only ever complained about something being unfair once when I was a kid. Once was enough. A well-meaning family friend heard me complaining that someone was cheating while we were playing soccer in the neighborhood. I still remember her pulling me aside, her words stinging like a wasp.

Andi, you know what's unfair? That your brother will never be able to walk. He doesn't ever get to play soccer. That's a big deal. That's unfair. This is child's play. Your parents don't need to deal with your whining. Figure it out yourself.

Every time I think about something being unfair, I always return to that moment. Of course, I knew Benj was different. He wasn't walking, but I didn't know he wasn't ever going to walk. Not until that moment. When Mrs. Cheney said that my whole world shifted on its axis. Benj is six years younger than me. I was probably about ten, which made him four. Whenever I'd asked Mom or Dad about it before that point, they said he hadn't read the book on development and was on his own schedule.

That made sense to me, because what baby can read a book?

Later that night, I straight up asked Mom if Benj was ever going to walk or play soccer. That's when she told me he had this thing called Spinal Muscular Atrophy—SMA—and no, he wasn't ever going to walk. She told me he was going to be getting an electric wheelchair when he went to school, and that we would be building a new house that would be accessible for Benj.

I nodded along like I knew what that meant. I didn't want to ask my mom any more questions, when this was obviously so hard for her to talk about. I decided in that moment that I'd never stress my mom out again.

We moved a few months later to be closer to the hospital, and I never saw Mrs. Cheney again. But her words echo in my brain all the time.

Figure it out yourself.

I should get that tattooed on my body.

I think about texting Benj, but I can talk about it tomorrow when I surprise him. I'm flying out of Logan on the 7 a.m. flight, which will put me there in time for lunch, barring any flight delays.

Until then, I'll work on how to figure this out myself.

I wasn't looking forward to the early morning flight when I booked it, but with it being such last minute, I didn't have much of a choice. Now I'm thankful for it. My alarm is set for 3:30 a.m., which gives me enough time to shower, brush my teeth, and head to the airport. It'll still be dark and the T won't be running, so I've already scheduled an Uber to get me there.

I can always sleep on the plane.

That's what will have to happen because sleep certainly isn't finding me now. Thoughts are swirling around my brain, causing my heart rate to spike and cold sweat to break out across my chest. I lie there, staring at the ceiling, my eyes wide open.

When the adrenaline rushing through my veins doesn't permit sleep to come, I try the next strategy—opening ClikClak and mindlessly scrolling.

After a bit, I stumble across a parody of a sportscaster calling dogs at the dog park as if it were a major sporting event. They're hilarious, and I find myself watching the entire playlist. I don't know who this person is, but she needs to be in the business. She's more entertaining than some of the ex-athletes they hire to be on TV.

@HannahLaRosa

After I finish the Dog Park playlist, I start watching some of her other videos. Her most recent shows the Eiffel Tower.

I'd kill to be in Paris right now. I'd kill multiple people to be there officiating the Global Games. I'm guessing murder won't help my case with the USSLRA though. I can practically hear Nathan. *Well, this is what happens when we let hysterical women with raging hormones into the league—they just can't control themselves.*

Okay, this line of thought will not be productive. Back to Hannah's ClikClaks of Paris. The video is a photo montage. I have to watch it several times for my brain to be able to process all the information my eyes are seeing. In addition to the traditional Paris landmarks and French cuisine, she's got pictures from the Global Games. Specifically, the ones the US played in.

Then there's a picture of her wearing a jersey with the name "Entay" on the back. That's the US National Team's goalie, Callaghan Entay. Funny, I wouldn't have pictured this girl for a cleat chaser. Not that I know her at all. I'm simply judging by her content.

And I was right. She's not a soccer groupie. She's legit dating Callaghan Entay.

The last picture is of them on the plane back to the States. Over it is text that says, "The US may have lost, but I certainly won. Stay tuned for big news coming soon."

Aww, I'm guessing they're engaged. I click on Entay's ClikClak to see, but there's just generic coverage from the games, and one repost of the picture of his girlfriend wearing his jersey.

A quick glance at the clock shows it's after one, and my window to sleep has long passed. I continue my deep dive on ClikClak, specifically Hannah LaRosa's profile.

She's really good at this social media thing. Plus, she knows sports—soccer specifically.

I'm not sure if it's desperation or sleep deprivation, or maybe a little of both, but I send her a message.

> @Andi: Hi Ms. LaRosa, My name is Andi Nichols. I stumbled across your profile, and I wanted to tell you your dog park series is brilliant. I can see you having a great career in broadcasting. I was wondering if you ever do

consulting to help people build a positive reputation on ClikClak? There's a relatively unflattering video of me making the rounds, and it has real potential to negatively impact my career. Would you have any suggestions for how to counteract that effect? Thanks in advance!

I don't have to wait too long before my phone vibrates, indicating I've got a new message.

@HannahLaRosa: THE Andi Nichols?

I have to smile. I'm not looking for fame or celebrity status, but I do want people to know the work I've done. I can't believe she knows who I am.

@Andi: The one and the same. And I'm sorry this is so late. I didn't think you'd answer.

Her response is immediate.

@HannahLaRosa: Sleep is for the weak. My body doesn't know what time zone it's in anyway. Brandon needs some sense slapped into him. He's seriously a PR nightmare. I would not want to be his agent.

I'm glad I'm not the only one who thinks that. I'm not sure that even the best agent and PR team could spin him into a likable guy.

@HannahLaRosa: Sometime I'll have to tell you about the time he kidnapped me.

Okay, now I need to know more. I put his name into the search bar.

An hour later, I'm quite convinced that Brandon Nix is exactly who I thought he was—on and off the field. I really can't believe that Nathan would think I had anything to do with the likes of him. Nathan obviously doesn't know me very well.

Not many people do. I'm a closed book.

That's what Mike said when he asked for the divorce. That I was a closed book, and he was no longer interested in reading it.

Yeah, those words still sting.

Not to mention he had already picked up a trashy magazine from the USSLRA headquarters.

I mean, he wasn't wrong, but no one wants to hear that. It's not like I don't know that I'm … standoffish. I've worked hard on that. I mean, look at what's happening now. If I were to show more emotions or passion or even reactions, can you imagine what would be said then?

I was literally standing there like a statue while Brandon Nix screamed in my face, and it's been sexualized. What is wrong with our society?

And what is wrong with Brandon Nix? There's a video of him outside practice today, his hair in its stupid man bun, making duck faces at whoever was filming him. Ugh, and he winked too. And no surprise, he drives a souped-up fancy sports car. He's about as clichéd as you can get.

I bet he has a small penis.

Actually, there's footage of him jumping rope in gray sweatpants which supports just the opposite. Doesn't matter. You know he's got diseases.

He is what's wrong with our society: because of his ability to kick a ball, we value him. We'll overlook all the faults, like the temper and the womanizing, and the lack of an internal filter, just because he's physically fit and somewhat attractive.

Okay, pretty attractive, if you got rid of the hair.

I get the sociology and biological drive behind it. Men who were strong and healthy were found to be more desirable to mate with to carry on the species. But we have to have evolved from there, right? The whole idea of the alpha male leaves nothing but distaste in my mouth, and Brandon Nix is the prime example of an alpha male. No, thank you.

But now, without sleep having crossed my path, it's time to get up and put myself together to go to the airport. As the excitement of getting to see my brother takes over, all thoughts of Brandon Nix slip from my brain.

That's the way it should be.

CHAPTER 8: BRANDON

I stare at my phone, blinking in disbelief.

Jess: OMG, B, it's amazing out here. I've never been this happy in all my life. I've found my home

Most people would be happy to receive this message from their sister. Most people would be happy for their sister. I am not most people, mostly because of my sister.

I don't waste time with pleasantries or beating around the bush.

Me: Are you high?

Jess: High on life

That is not the flippant answer I want to hear. Of course, no answer she gives me will be good enough. That's the problem with having an addict in your life. There's no trust, and I can't think of one scenario in which there will be again.

Me: Uh-huh

Jess: No, really. Wyoming is the most beautiful place in the world. You have to come see me, and then you'll understand

Me: Let me guess, you need money

Money, jail, and rehab are the only reasons Jess ever reaches out to me.

Jess: B, no. I'm doing really well. You have to see it for yourself. I've had a breakthrough

Me: What's his name?

Jess: Her name

Me: Ok, what's her name?

Jess: Her name is Thunder

Jesus, what kind of mess is she getting herself into now? Is Jess's new girlfriend a stripper or a hooker? No way Jess can keep clean in that lifestyle.

Me: What kind of name is that?

A picture pops up on my screen, showing Jess, her face tanned and freckled, with strands of her braided hair whipping across her face. Her arms are around the neck of a massive black horse.

Me: That's Thunder?

Jess: Isn't she gorgeous? And she loves me too. You have to meet her

Something small twitches in my chest. If I didn't know better, I'd say it was the beginning of hope. Hope that this time, it takes for Jess. Hope that she really is better. Hope that she will live.

I can't let myself hope though. I've hoped too much in the past.

The only thing hope leads to is disappointment. It's one reason why I'm so frank with people. No need to blow smoke up their ass and give them hope for something that's not going to happen.

Yet here I am, hoping that the smiling woman in the picture is real. I click back on it. She's gained a little weight, which is a good thing. She has color, though that's probably from days spent out in the sun. Her eyes do look clear though. They're bright. They don't have that hollowed vacant look that plagued her for years.

But pictures can be altered. They can be fake. They can be staged. I can't believe it though. Not yet. At least not until I see it with my own eyes. Without another thought, I quickly search for a flight to Jackson, Wyoming. I book a rental car to drive me to her ranch, which appears to be about an hour away.

I won't be able to rest until I do this.

I can fly back in a day or two, after I make sure she's okay. I send a quick text to Coach Janssen saying I have to go out of town for family reasons. I don't think I've ever taken personal time before, so there shouldn't be a problem. I'll get in a run and a workout while I'm out there, so I really won't be missing anything. Two days tops and I'll be back at practice with the peace of mind knowing Jess is okay.

I don't *quite* pay attention to the time of the flight when I book it until after all is said and done. I'm on a 7 a.m. plane to Jackson Hole, and I'll take the red-eye back on Wednesday. There isn't a flight directly to Jackson Hole, so I've got a layover somewhere. Whatever. I'll still get there in the end.

Those times suck. I am not a morning person, so it's predictably hard for me to get up in time to make it to the airport and catch my flight. I barely have time to shower. My hair hangs in waves, dripping water down my T-shirt. It'll dry by the time I land.

There's no easy way to get to Logan from where I am, other than driving north to Boston and then hanging a right. Luck is on my side because it's practically night still, with the sun just popping up over the horizon, bright red in the haze of the July sky. I make the trek in under 30 minutes, which would never happen later in the day.

Even with that luck on my side, it takes me forever to get through security. With my hair down and casual shorts and flip-flops on, no one recognizes me until I reach security and they check my name.

Then, it's a thing, and the guard wants pictures. I let her take one, ignoring her hand which is definitely lower than my waist before practically sprinting through the terminal. If I wasn't running late, I'd probably take a second look. No time for that now.

I picked the wrong day to wear flip-flops.

I reach down and pull them off. Much better.

I break into a run as I hear my flight paged. For most people, this would be a struggle, but it's a warm-up for me. I make it to the gate as they announce, "Final call for Passenger Nix on Flight 647. This is the final call." I slow to a walk as I flash the boarding pass on my phone. I'm not even winded.

Now that I know I made it, I stroll down the gangway to the plane, ducking as I enter. My seat is in first class so I don't have to walk far. I pop my bag in the overhead and sit down. A minute later my earbuds are in and one of my favorite playlists is streaming through my ears. I close my eyes and don't plan on opening them until I have to change planes. That should give me a good four more hours of sleep.

As I start to doze off, I think about the whirlwind the last twelve hours have been since Jess texted me. If I can just see for myself that she's okay, maybe I'll finally be able to relax. Maybe I can settle down and stop being so hot-headed. It doesn't take a rocket scientist—or a psychologist like Watson Ross—to figure out that a lot of my stress is because of my family.

Since I can't take it out on them, I take it out on my opponents on the field. It's a coping mechanism that's worked for me for as long as I can remember. But if I can get this family shit settled, maybe I'll finally be less angry. Then, if I'm less angry, I'll draw less penalties. I won't be on probation anymore, and the Buzzards will have to start recognizing me for my contributions to the team.

When my contract is up, I can negotiate for a larger salary. My life is finally coming together. Just as long as this trip goes exactly how I need it to.

CHAPTER 9: ANDI

I hate running late. I'm sure it doesn't take a lot of analysis to figure out why. We were always late. My mom never could accurately calculate how long it would take her to get Benj ready and loaded up into the car. Or how long it would take to tie down his wheelchair once he was in the van. Or how long it would take to back into the handicapped parking space because some asshat parked on the striped lines meaning Benj couldn't unload on the passenger side like he was supposed to.

It didn't matter, because we were always dashing in at the last minute. I wanted to shrink into the floor every time that happened. We got enough stares and gawks simply because Benj was in a wheelchair. Like that was all they saw—a wheelchair. I can still feel everyone looking at us. I didn't need any more cause for a scene by entering late too.

As an adult, promptness is of utmost importance. I will never again be on the receiving end of the stares of those who were on time. I try to give them grace and all that, but it's my Achilles' heel.

It hits too close to home, so it's easier to feel annoyed by the person making their grand entrance after the prescribed start time than to deal with all those feelings I had growing up.

I can take all my unresolved emotions and project them right onto the person who doesn't have their shit together enough to make it on time.

Like the man getting on the plane now.

We were supposed to push off five minutes ago, but they held us for this guy. I don't see much as he saunters on, except for a flash of long hair that used to be dark but has been on the receiving end of too much bleach. I really don't like long hair on guys. I know, to each his own, but it's definitely not a personal preference of mine.

He moves as if he hasn't a care in the world. Certainly, no worries that he's had us all waiting. It doesn't matter to him that I'm anxious for this flight to take off so it can land so I can finally get to see my brother.

Now that Mr. Important has finally settled in his first-class seat—figures—I return my attention to my laptop. I might as well bang out some work while we fly. The more I get done now, the more uninterrupted time I'll have with Benj.

My plan, which seemed ideal when I made it, did not account for the screaming toddler next to me. Even with my noise-canceling earbuds in, the cacophony is distracting. As are the child's feet, which kick and thrash constantly. More than once my laptop skitters off the tray table.

I'd be annoyed, but the mother looks so frazzled. Poor woman. I'm sure this isn't how she wanted to travel. I take a deep breath, willing myself to tune out the son of Satan and his blood-curdling screaming. It works—almost—until the toddler goes ramrod straight, extending his arms straight over his head, and dumping the contents of his sippy cup on my lap.

And my laptop.

I jump up, holding my computer, trying to shake the chocolate milk off it before it can seep in and fry the electrical components. The mother apologizes profusely, tears welling up in her eyes.

Certainly, I'm annoyed, but I can't let her see. She's taking this hard enough. This isn't her fault. Kids are unpredictable. Or predictable in not doing what you want them to do. I give her a tight-lipped smile and assure her I'm fine. A flight attendant rushes over with some towels to help mop up the mess.

I'm drenched. Who knew those cups could hold so much? Why wasn't the top secured in the first place? And because it's milk, I can practically smell the rancid foul odor that will no doubt be wafting off me by the time we land in Denver.

No biggie. I can take this in stride. If I can just get to my carry on, I can change my clothes. I tell this to the attendant, as well as the harried mother.

"Let me just pull my bag down, and I can change. It's fine." Okay, maybe my tone is the *teensiest* bit on the clipped side, but I don't let my irritation show. The flight attendant rewards my lack of negative response because she says, "Why don't you come up front and use the bathroom up here? It's a little more spacious in first class, so it'll be easier for you to change in. I think we have a seat up there as well, and you can spend the remainder of the flight there."

Sometimes it pays to stuff all your feelings way down deep.

I thank her for her thoughtfulness and proceed to yank my bag down from the overhead bin. Now I'm fit and flexible, with agility being a necessary part of my job, but changing my clothes in an airplane bathroom seems like it requires the skill of a circus contortionist. I have to leave my suitcase outside and pull out the first clothes I find, which are a pair of ratty sweatpants and an oversized T-shirt that says, "Caution: This Physical Therapist is easily distracted by your awful gait pattern." It's a leftover from my college days and hasn't seen the light of day as anything but pajamas in at least a decade.

It's fine. Definitely worth going through to get the upgrade. Plus, Benj will think this is funny when I see him. He has a warped sense of humor. Much better than mine. I got muscles that work; he got all the personality.

The flight attendant takes my bag to stow in a closet and guides me a few rows back where there's an open window seat. A window seat that's next to an aisle seat that's currently occupied by the Neanderthal that delayed our flight.

Now that I'm standing less than a foot away, I recognize the bleach-blond locks immediately.

His hair is even worse up close. Has he never heard of conditioner? I bet he's one of those guys who uses a 3-in-1 shampoo, conditioner, and body wash. Yuck.

But no, it doesn't stop there. His head is tipped down, his chin practically resting on his chest. I expect him to shift or move or something to let me pass, but he remains still. I clear my throat. Nothing. The flight attendant says, "Excuse me, sir." Nothing. She shakes his shoulder slightly. Still nothing.

Then, a rumbling sound emanates from the man's mouth, rising in a crescendo to one of the loudest snores I've ever heard. His head lifts, as if the vibrations emitted by his obstructed airway created their own forcefield strong enough to lift his head and all of that stupid Fabio hair.

As this happens, his stupid Fabio hair parts like a curtain, exposing his face. A face I recognize. A face I loathe.

A face that belongs to Brandon Nix.

I'd rather sit next to the demon child.

I turn to the flight attendant. "You know, on second thought, I'll just go back to my seat. I'm sure it's fine." I brush past her and head through the curtains to where the common folk sit.

That was close.

Except when I get back to my row, the toddler is now stretched out across my seat, fast asleep. His mother's eyes are wide with panic. I may not have kids of my own, but even I know not to wake a sleeping baby. Especially not one with the lung capacity that this one has.

"Is there anywhere else I can sit?" I look around. Surely there's got to be another empty seat.

"I'm afraid the only other unoccupied seat is the one in first class."

I look from my former seat to the front of the plane. I can't disturb this kid. But I don't know how I'm going to sit next to the man who may have cost me my career either.

I see tears again in the exhausted mother's eyes. There's no choice. Not really. Not without making a scene and becoming public enemy number one. I make my way back up to the front of the plane, clenching my molars together.

He's still asleep. The beast is practically sprawled out now, one leg in the aisle and the other taking up all available space in front of his seat. He's the poster child for manspreading. His head is back against the headrest now, tipped slightly to the side, with a small trickle of drool puddling at the corner of his open mouth.

Eww.

Also, this is a legit fear of mine with sleeping on a plane. I've trained myself to doze off with my fist pressed to my mouth to prevent the drool from escaping.

He's still snoring.

The flight attendant looks at me sheepishly before turning to Sleeping Beauty. "Excuse me, sir." She taps his shoulder. Brandon Nix doesn't move. At this rate, I'm going to be here all day.

"It's fine." I think I've used that word more times in the last ten minutes than I have in the last ten years. For the record, none of this is fine, but I don't need anyone else to feel bad about things they can't control. I place one hand on Brandon's headrest and the other on the back of the seat in front of him. In a maneuver worthy of a gymnastics gold medal, I manage to lift and shift myself over the ogre's massive thighs without waking him.

I'm now sweating, but at least Prince Foul-mouth wasn't disturbed. Knowing how he acts when he's awake, I can only imagine the litany of rage I'd be in for if I woke him right now. I plop into my seat and exhale. What is the luck that Brandon Nix would be on my plane?

My luck. The worst kind.

But I shouldn't complain. He's simply another passenger on the same flight as me. I mean, the odds of this are extremely low, but not zero. That's what my dad would always say when talking about my brother's health or treatment options or potential surgeries. I guess when your child is born with a disease that only affects 1 in 100,000 people, low odds mean nothing.

So this is nothing. A mere blip. A slight inconvenience. Nothing more. I can shove down all my feelings of animosity toward the human sitting next to me for the next four hours, and then it will be in the past. I won't have to worry about Brandon Nix until the next time I see him on the pitch.

CHAPTER 10: BRANDON

I'm dreaming the plane has hit turbulence, and we're going to crash.

Oh shit, it's not a dream.

I'm jolted awake as the plane bounces through the air like a toddler on a trampoline full of drunk adults. I grab whatever I can, which is the armrest to my left and a person to my right.

Weird. I could have sworn that seat was empty when we took off.

Then I feel fingers prying my hand off. "Let go of me!"

I try to glance over, but we hit another big bump. I close my eyes as my head slams back into my seat. I'm going to die. Immediately my thoughts jump to my mother.

Is this what Mom felt like as the truck barreled toward her? Did she know? At least I'll get to see her again soon.

I hope. I haven't been the best behaved, but I'm sure God understands what I've had to deal with.

"This is your captain speaking. We've hit a bit of turbulence—"

No shit, Sherlock. What's your next case?

"—due to a strong front of powerful storms moving in. We tried flying north to circumvent but the front has shifted slightly. We have to land until this passes. There are several severe weather warnings in effect, and we will need to land now. Crew, please prepare."

"What the actual fuck?" I growl as the plane jerks again. I'd like to let out a few more choice words, but the plane starts a rapid descent, and I've no choice but to squeeze my eyes shut and hold on for dear life.

There's a pretty good chance I'm going to puke all over myself.

A few minutes of hell with my stomach rising up into my throat only to drop to my toes and repeat and then we're on the ground.

"I said, let go!" The voice next to me permeates through the fog of fear that is currently engulfing me. I finally open my eyes and turn my head to see a woman sitting next to me.

Okay, I'm *sure* she wasn't there when I fell asleep. She's looking at me through narrowed eyes. The rest of her face remains expressionless, but I'm pretty sure she's giving me a death glare. She's holding her hand as if my touch burned it.

Wait, she looks a little familiar.

Not a little familiar. A lot familiar.

Fuck no.

"Wait, aren't you that lady ref?" Her blonde hair is down, but I'm pretty sure it's her. I remember that icy blue stare.

She rolls her eyes. "I have a name. Andi Nichols."

"You threw me out of the game."

"You threw yourself out, Brandon Nix. I simply called and penalized the infractions as I saw them. And that was totally a handball. Don't even try to argue. Again."

"Most refs would have let it slide. And then it wouldn't have been my second yellow."

"Most refs are lazy and don't want people mad at them, especially big baby soccer players. People are mad at me for existing. I could have called a perfect game, and someone would still find something to gripe about simply because I'm a woman. And we both know that the penalty against Treyvon Wallis-Smalls could easily have been a red card by itself."

She *may* have a point. "You weren't sitting here the whole time, were you?" I change the subject rather than let her know that I agree with her. For the record, I didn't disagree with her because she's a woman. I'm just pissed I got sent off and am now on probation for it. I'd feel this pissed off if she had a dick. "I would have remembered that."

"How many concussions have you had? Of course I wasn't here the whole time."

Damn, she's snippy. "What crawled up your butt?"

Her mouth opens and then closes. She repeats this, resembling a fish. I take this as an opening. "Do you know I'm on probation with the Buzzards? All because of you."

The captain interrupts my rant. "We are temporarily grounded in Appleton, Wisconsin. We'll deplane and move to a weather-sheltered area in the airport until the front passes. We will continue to update about plans to continue the flight at a later time."

We've finally taxied to a stop, and I stand to get my luggage from the overhead bin.

The lady ref stands but remains hunched over due to the height of the bulkhead. She looks like a bum, in oversized sweatpants that have bleach stains down the front and a large shapeless T-shirt. Combined with her socks and Birkenstocks, she looks like she's just rolled out of bed.

She takes in a breath and then lets it out slowly. She says something, but I can't hear her. The noise level of the passengers is exceedingly loud. Probably because we almost died and now we're all stranded— where are we again?

"Listen, I don't need your bullshit about how I need to check my behavior on the field. I'm there to do a job, and I get the job done. I'm the leading scorer." I take a step back so she can move into the aisle. The doors are still closed, so we're packed in like sardines.

She stands straight up and we're almost eye to eye. There's barely any space in between our bodies.

"A truly good soccer player can figure out how to score goals without fouls."

The door opens and she turns to face it. The passengers in front of us begin to file out, creating space between our bodies. The flight attendant hands the lady ref her suitcase. She takes it and then turns over her shoulder. "And this is just a hint, but maybe you want to invest in some breath mints."

Then she's gone, leaving me standing there in shock.

Someone nudges me from behind, startling me back into reality. This is a nightmare. It cannot be happening.

But it is.

Not only did we have to make an emergency landing due to the weather, but now we're *here*. I'm not even sure where here is. The only other time I've ever been to Wisconsin is when we played the Milwaukee Steins.

Yes, their soccer club is named after a beer stein.

I don't remember that airport being as tiny as this one. So tiny that there is one person working the United Airlines counter. There are four people ahead of me, one being Andi Nichols. I guess I'm not the only one who wants to see what the plan is for moving forward.

Nobody insults me and gets away with it.

I'm about to tell her exactly what I think of her when my phone pings. It's an update from the airline, indicating that I should remain close to the terminal to listen for updated information as it becomes available.

It pings again. That was quick.

Nope, it's my sister.

Jess: What time are you getting in? I'm so excited to see you

I hum with frustration.

Me: Emergency landing in Podunk, Wisconsin. Apparently bad storms moving through. Hopefully can get back in air soon

"Can you stop?" *She* has turned around and is now glaring. There's no mistaking it.

"Stop what?" I'm just standing here, texting my sister.

"You're growling like a bear. Or maybe a disgruntled badger. We are in Wisconsin."

If it were any other woman slinging this insult, I'd probably turn it around into a flirtation. Seeing as how it's Andi Nichols, I'd rather hit on a bear. Or a badger.

I'm sure either would be friendlier.

A loud clap of thunder rattles the windows of the terminal as rain begins to pelt. We both pause our momentary arguing to look at Mother Nature's fury.

It's unsettling to watch from the safety of the airport. I can't imagine what flying through this would be like. It may be inconvenient, but I'm glad we landed.

"Is this going to mess up your day?" I ask Andi without looking at her. I don't know why I ask. I'm not one for small talk, and she's the last person I want to be making it with.

In the minute that it takes her to answer, I sneak a glance to see her expression. I wish I hadn't. "What?" Her nose wrinkles in disgust, as if talking to me is beneath her.

"Cool your jets, Andrew. I was just being polite." I don't know where that name came from, but I like it. If I had to put her number in my phone—which I cannot ever see myself doing—that's how I'd save it. I smile a little at the thought.

Sometimes, it's the little things.

CHAPTER 11: ANDI

A *ndrew?*

Why the heck would he call me that?

"It's Andi. As in Andrea."

"Whatever you say, Andrew." With that, Brandon Nix walks away.

How dare he? I mean, I wasn't the most pleasant with him either, but still. Andrew? Me likening him to a badger was appropriate. He was certainly making animalistic noises for no apparent reason.

I wonder if he plays soccer because he doesn't have opposable thumbs to otherwise throw and catch a ball. It would explain a lot.

I cannot believe my luck to be on this doomed flight with the very man who may be responsible for putting my career in jeopardy. What did I ever do to deserve this?

And why does this man get a rise out of me? I don't normally let my feelings make their way to the surface. I've never wanted to burden my family with my emotions, since they had so much to deal with, with my brother. That skill has served me well as a referee. I can't afford to let my feelings show in my line of work. But now that there's no audience, I didn't think twice about letting that oaf know what I thought of him.

No poker face here.

I step up to the counter to ask for an estimated timeframe to landing in Denver. The harried clerk types away on the keyboard. "I'm afraid it might be a while. Apparently, a tornado touched down outside of metro Denver, and Denver International was impacted. They're closed to flights for the moment."

"A tornado? In Denver? I thought it was next to impossible because of the mountains." I shake my head. That can't be right.

She shrugs. "I guess it's pretty rare but can happen. I mean, what are the odds?"

There's that question again.

The pang hits my stomach with such a visceral force that it's all I can do not to double over. What are the odds? And what if it touched down by my parents' home? It's not like Benj can run to the basement.

My fingers fumble my phone as I pull it out of my sweatpants pocket. They don't seem to be working, and my phone falls to the floor. I squat to pick it up, but there's a hand on it already.

"I'd expect you to have more coordination than to drop your phone, Andrew."

"Andi."

"Here ya go, Andrew," Brandon Nix says, handing me my phone back. I snatch it out of his hands and turn around, cradling it as Sméagol did with his precious in *Lord of the Rings*.

> Me: Are you okay?
> Benj: Fine, why?

My body sags with relief.

> Me: Tornado in Denver?
> Benj: Really? Can't believe I missed it
> Me: How did you miss it?
> Benj: I'm in Albuquerque

Albuquerque? What the hell is he doing there?

> Me: What are you doing there? How did you get there?
> Benj: I'm road-tripping

Wait? What is going on? I feel like I'm in a fever dream or something. Maybe that's what all this is! Maybe I'm really asleep on the plane which is still in the air and Brandon Nix wasn't even on the plane.

Why was he there? I'm not sure if I'm more disturbed by running into him like this or the thought that I'm dreaming about him. A shudder runs through my body.

> Me: How are you road tripping?
> Benj: I'm hitchhiking. Is it still hiking if you can't walk? Hitchrolling? I've only run into one possible serial killer so far. My goal is 3.

He thinks he's hilarious.

> Me: No seriously

Benj: I am serious. Don't worry, I'd just roll away. My battery is long lasting, so I can keep going even when they get tired.

Me: You're not funny

Benj: Of course I am. What's up with you? How are you spending your downtime, other than working and watching Global Games because you are the job?

Should I tell him? I don't want to make him feel bad. But also, why didn't he say anything to me about going?

Me: I thought I'd come and see you, but my plane almost crashed because of the storm and now you're not there. I can't believe neither you nor Mom nor Dad told me you guys would be away

There's a moment before his response comes in.

Benj: Don't go ballistic

His words have me immediately ready to go ballistic.

Me: Do I ever?

Benj: Not outwardly, but you internally freak out

See? My brother really does know me the best.

Me: I'm waiting and totally not freaking out at all

Benj: That means you are

Damn it. I hate it that my brother is always right.

Benj: I'm with my girlfriend. Before you lose your shit, we've been talking for about 2 years now. She's come to visit multiple times.

We planned this trip out to see as much of the country as we can. I have a bucket list you know and let's be real: I don't have all the time in the world. We have an accessible van and we're seeing the nation. I was going to tell you when we head east, but I know you're busy. I was going to surprise you.

I have to sit down to digest this news. I want to be happy for my brother. I *should* be happy for him. This is a very normal thing for a thirty-something to do.

But he's not on a normal trajectory.

I'm not trying to be ableist or mean. He's already outlived the grim lifespan he was originally expected to have. There've been some new therapies that have slowed the progress of his disease. He's the first generation with his condition to live this long. I know this, and I agree that he should do as much as he can.

But have they thought through the logistics? What if something happens to his wheelchair? What if the hotels aren't accessible? Who's transferring him? Is it his girlfriend? Is she doing his toileting and feeding too? Benj doesn't have much strength, and his joints are pretty contracted. Feeding, bathing, dressing—oh my God, has she seen him naked? She must have.

But any girlfriend would. That's normal. I mean, I don't think Benj spent a lot of time thinking about me getting naked with Mike when we were married, but you know it happened.

I guess I never thought about it happening for Benj. I'm happy that it has but ... why would he keep this from me?

He's supposed to be my person. The person I tell everything to. Why doesn't he feel the same way about me? I guess I always figured he didn't have much to say because he didn't have much going on. I didn't pry because I didn't want him to feel isolated.

Except now that's how I feel.

I always thought Benj and I were a team. Even if I wasn't there physically, I texted him daily. Multiple times a day.

Even now, he didn't tell me her name.

He doesn't want me to know.

I have never felt so alone as I do right this second.

"Why the long face, Andrew?"

Of course, the bane of my existence is back, as if today could not get worse.

"Leave me alone," I mutter.

"What? What's that? I couldn't hear you." He cups his hand to his ear. I am not in the mood for him. When I don't respond, he plops down in the chair next to me. Swell.

I continue to ignore him. I've got too much on my mind to waste energy on him. I can't believe Benj isn't in Colorado. In one way, I'm relieved I don't have to worry about him making it through a random tornado. That's certainly one contingency plan we never practiced.

Then it dawns on me that even if Benj is safe, it doesn't mean my parents are. I sit up quickly, frantically trying to FaceTime them. My mom answers after what feels like forever.

Unless she has some green screen background—which is way beyond her technological level—they're not in Colorado either. "Um ... where are you?"

"We're in Aruba! Benjamin bought us this trip. It's a three-week Caribbean cruise. He said we deserved to get away while he was traveling."

"Yeah, about that, Mom—"

"Oh, don't start, Andi. Benjamin said he'd tell you when the timing was right. He was afraid you'd get all—well, you know how you get."

There is no way to take this that isn't insulting. But, since I'm my own worst critic, I have about a million things running through my brain that this could mean. I'm gonna need some clarification.

"And what do you mean by that?"

"Andi, you tend to be overprotective. A little too much. You'd get worried and try to fix problems that aren't yours. Samantha and Benjamin are quite capable of handling this trip on their own."

I don't say anything. I certainly don't tell Mom she hit it right on the nose about my reaction. "So, it's probably not a great time for me to visit you in Colorado then."

As I say this, the loudspeaker blares that there will be information about my flight in a few minutes. I see the look on Mom's face. "Were you going to come out and see us soon? We'll be back next week."

I have a game in Birmingham next week. I send them my schedule regularly, but Benj is the only one who ever reads it. "I'll have to check and see. Maybe soon."

"Where are you now?"

For the first time since we had this emergency landing, I'm relieved. I don't have to lie to her. "Wisconsin."

"Okay, well safe travels. Talk to you soon. Hugs and kisses." She air-kisses and then hangs up.

Well, this is just great.

CHAPTER 12: BRANDON

I'd say this day can't get any worse, but I haven't seen the state my sister is in yet. I'll reserve judgment for when I get to Jackson Hole. Or wherever she is in the middle of nowhere.

Andrew here—I make myself laugh—doesn't seem to be having a great day either. I wasn't trying to eavesdrop, but she was on FaceTime, so what was I supposed to do?

It's kind of shitty that her parents didn't tell her they were away, but it sounds like she didn't tell them she was coming either. Serves her right.

I text my sister.

> *Me: Hit a delay with the weather. I'll send you my ETA when I have that information*

What time is it anyway? We left Boston around seven. My phone says it's almost ten. Does that mean ten here? Or ten in Boston? I have no idea how long we were even flying for. The thing I hate most about travel is the time zone thing. I can never figure it out.

I google "what time is it in Boston?" It's almost eleven there, so my phone must have automatically updated.

But it's been at least five minutes, and there's no answer from Jess. I try not to read anything into the fact that she doesn't respond. It doesn't mean she's up to no good. She might be out in the fields or in a barn or something. I don't really know what she's doing out there. I try not to let my imagination get the best of me.

So I distract myself by listening to Andi's phone conversation and otherwise looking over her shoulder to see what she's doing on her phone.

"Didn't anyone ever tell you it's rude to look at someone else's phone?" she says in a huff, moving over one seat.

"I don't worry myself with what other people think of me." It's true. They're going to think the worst no matter what, so why bother? "You should try it sometime."

Her phone signals an incoming FaceTime call. She swears under her breath before answering it, her eyes rolling. But then the oddest thing happens. As she accepts, it's as if a mask descends over her features and a banal smile forms on her mouth. "Hi, Mike, what's up?"

"Where are you? Did you get the money thing straightened out? Don't tell Nate I told you what we make per game. I don't think we're supposed to talk about it. I don't need to get on his shit list. You know, you probably shouldn't bring it up either. Not if you want more games. He seems like the type to hold a grudge."

The distance between seats means I can't see who it is, but I can definitely hear. He's talking about games. Is it someone I know?

She sighs slightly. "I didn't bring it up, and I'm probably not going to. I can't. I'm on thin ice as it is." Her eyes dart to me. Of course, I'm not even pretending that I'm not hanging on every word. She makes a hand gesture, shooing me away.

If that's what she wants, she's got it. I stand up and begin to walk down the aisle. As soon as I see her gaze return to her phone screen, I double back, walking behind her row of chairs. As I come up behind her, I lean in.

Mike Barnaby. He's a tool. He's also one of the refs in the USSL. I guess it only makes sense that they talk. "Hi, Mike!" I wave, grinning like a fool. "How's it going?"

I see his mouth drop open in the millisecond before she ends the call. She stands up and, in the iciest tone I've ever heard, says, "Do you know what you just did? You just ruined my career."

"All I did was say hi to Mike Barnaby. That guy's a total tool."

She immediately begins pacing. She's muttering to herself. Every so often, she looks over at me and glares.

"Andrew, calm down. It's not the end of the world."

The look on her face says that it is. "I ... I cannot ... How could you? He's gonna tell them we were together."

"We're not together. We just happen to be in the same place. It's no big deal. And why does he care, other than he's a jackwad? He the jealous type?"

She lets out a bitter laugh. "Not with me. Not since the divorce."

Andrew here was married to Mike Barnaby? That's interesting. I can't picture them together. I step over the back of the chair and sit down, crossing one leg over the other. "Why don't you sit down and relax? I think they said we'd be boarding soon."

I run my hands through my hair and pull it back into a ponytail. Andi watches me, the bridge of her nose wrinkling ever so slightly. She's probably jealous of my luscious locks.

"Have you ever heard of conditioner? Your hair is fried."

Okay, maybe jealous isn't the right word. "I've never had any complaints before," I say with a sly grin.

Andi makes a little gagging motion. "Please don't," she says, holding up her hand. I'm about to ask *don't what* when a kid comes running up. He's maybe seven or eight and wearing a Boston Buzzards jersey. "Are you Brandon Nix?"

His father arrives a moment later, breathless. "Maverick, you can't bother this man."

I lean forward, putting my elbows on my knees and lacing my fingers together. "I am Brandon Nix."

"I told you, Dad," he says glancing back at his father. "You didn't believe me."

I nod sagely. "It's the hair. No one recognizes me when I wear it down. The minute I put it up ..."

Maverick is practically vibrating with excitement. "You're the Boston Buzzards' leading scorer! But you get kicked out too much. You should stop drawing penalties. Did you know your penalty cost your team the semifinals last year?"

I hear a dampened laugh come from next to me.

"Actually, it's the goalkeeper's job to stop the penalty kicks," I reply.

"And it's your job to make them." This kid pulls no punches. I glance up at his father whose face is beet red.

"Would you like a picture or not?" I huff. I glance over at Andi who's turned away and practically eating her fist, her shoulders shaking. "This is Andi Nichols. She's a referee for the USSL. You should get a picture with her too since apparently you know all the rules."

Andi's glare of death is back, but it disappears the minute she turns to face the kid and his father. I do not envy that man at all. He's got his hands full. Serves him right for naming his kid Maverick.

Pictures are done, and we're left standing there. Andi opens her mouth to say something, but we're interrupted by the announcement that they're ready to reboard our flight. Andi and I move toward the gate and board with the first-class passengers. We reach the row of our seats, and Andi arches her back as she hoists her suitcase above her head to the overhead bins. Her back presses to my front. Without thinking,

I reach up and guide it in, my arms forming a cage around hers.

"I don't need your help," she says with a huff as she sits down.

I fly so much, helping others with their luggage is a natural reaction. I'm only 5' 10", but I can bench press well over 200 pounds. In case you're wondering, at this point in the season, I'm about 165 pounds of pure muscle, so you have every right to be impressed. Lifting a suitcase up just helps speed along the boarding process.

"You don't have to get all snippy."

"And don't touch me." She plops down in her seat and puts her laptop and headphones in the seatback pocket.

"When did I touch you?" I'd think I'd remember touching her. She is so not my type. And the way she's dressed? She looks ridiculous. I'd never be interested in someone who takes so little interest in their appearance.

"You practically broke my hand when we were landing. You kept grabbing me."

Oh. That. I sit in my seat and buckle my seatbelt snuggly. "We were going down."

"It was just a bit of turbulence." She slides her earbuds in. I don't know if they're connected or not, but I get the message loud and clear.

Trust me, Andi Nichols. The feeling is mutual.

CHAPTER 13: ANDI

After what seems like the longest day known to man, I'm finally back in my apartment. The minute I landed in Denver, I practically sprinted off the plane and to the counter to get put on the next flight back to Boston.

Since my finances haven't changed since yesterday, I couldn't afford to upgrade myself to first class. I wasn't fortunate enough to get upgraded thanks to a cranky toddler either. Flying coach sucks.

I wish I could have enjoyed the full experience of flying in the lap of luxury. Instead, I cranked up the volume on my earbuds and tried to bury myself in work. I'd planned on reviewing at least four files. I didn't even get one completed. My attention was on Brandon.

Every move he made distracted me. Hell, his breathing distracted me. His snoring definitely did.

Seriously, how could he fall asleep so quickly and completely?

Not gonna lie, it's kind of impressive.

And maybe a tad envy producing.

That's neither here nor there. What matters is that *yet again* Brandon Nix got in my way. As long as Nathan doesn't pull me to cover any more Buzzards games this year, our paths won't cross, and my life will be better.

I trudge through my apartment door close to midnight. I can't believe that I left here at 4 a.m. today. That this all happened in the same one box on the calendar. This exhaustion has hit an all-new level. I don't bother digging my phone charger out of my bag before passing out on top of my duvet, still fully dressed.

The next thing I know, I jolt awake, not sure of what time it is, where I am, or even who I am. My eyes burn and feel like they're full of sawdust. My teeth are definitely fuzzy. It takes me a few minutes to orient.

I'm home. I look for my phone on the nightstand only to find it totally dead. Through a fog, I vaguely remember not wanting to put forth the effort to find my charger last night. Well, that was a poor decision.

I finally dig it out, plugging my phone in before sprinting to the bathroom. I am off my game, that's for sure. Yesterday seems like a bad dream. After finishing up in the bathroom, I wander around my apartment in a daze.

Did yesterday even happen? I'm not sure what the most unbelievable part of it was: the holy-terror child on the plane, getting moved next to Brandon Nix of all people, almost crashing, or finding out my brother has a whole secret life that I knew nothing about. Not to mention my parents are enjoying a tropical beach vacation.

I reach for my phone to re-read the text messages with Benj, if only to verify that this wasn't some sort of fever dream. But there are way too many notifications on my phone to deal with to ever even get to my brother's name.

What the holy hell?

I look at the clock. It's almost noon. I was only out for twelve hours. How could I have this many notifications? This cannot be good.

After verifying that none are from my family, I start to wade through. Something big must have happened.

I have over 100 ClikClak notifications, which is the most it will tell you at a time. It's been a few weeks since the video of the game went viral, so activity had died down on that platform. There must be a resurrection of that clip. You know, the one where Bad-Breath Brandon is screaming in my face?

Except ... that's not it. That's not it at all.

Oh, it still involves Brandon Nix. But this is worse. So much worse. Infinitely worse.

There's footage of us at the airport together. Of us posing with that kid. Of him putting my luggage in the overhead bins. And commentary on all of it.

Lots of commentary.

If people weren't speculating from that original video, they sure are now.

There are *hundreds* of videos of us. I mean, there are only two or three, but hundreds—maybe even thousands—of people have reposted or made their own content featuring it. There's no way this isn't going to get back to Nathan, if it hasn't already.

My career is over.

My hands shake as I flip over to my messages and my emails. Nothing from Nathan or the USSLRA. Yet. I'm sure it's only a matter of time.

If I'd eaten anything in the last 18 hours, there's no doubt I'd be vomiting it up. All because the spawn of Satan sitting next to me doused me in milk. I'm never drinking milk again.

I pace my apartment, running my hands through my hair as if that will solve the problem. Every time my phone dings, I jump, convinced that it will be the shoe dropping from Nathan. I'm in a cold sweat.

Good Lord, I smell.

I decide that maybe a long hot shower is what I need to relax and make myself feel better. Except I can't turn my mind off no matter what I do. So now I'm pruny and my hair is wet, and I don't have the faculties to dry and style it.

I mean, I never feel like styling it, which is why the slicked-back ponytails and braids I wear as a referee work great for me.

I stand there, in my towel, looking around my apartment for something—anything—that will give me a clue what to do next. Normally I'd text Benj, but I don't want to bother him on his trip. My parents for that matter either. I'm certainly *not* calling Mike.

I don't even have a pet to commiserate with. I travel too much to be able to care for another living creature.

I'm truly alone.

Alone and desperate.

Desperate times call for desperate measures, and if you looked up desperate in the dictionary, you'd be sure to see my picture, limp wet hair and all.

@Andi: You have a really big following on ClikClak right? Are you considered an influencer?

@HannahLaRosa: I wouldn't say influencer, but I have a decent-sized following. Why?

@Andi: Um, I seem to be a little viral again.

@HannahLaRosa: I see that. You and Brandon just can't seem to stay away from each other. <winky smiley face>

The thought of him fills me with rage. This is all his fault.

@Andi: That's just it. It was a coincidence. I swear.

@HannahLaRosa: Coincidence or not, the internet is shipping you hard.

As an elder millennial, I don't always understand what the young folks are talking about. Normally I try to hide the fact that I'm old and uncool, but there's no time for that now.

@Andi: Shipping?

@HannahLaRosa: You know, wanting you to be in a relationship.

Ew. Vomit.

@Andi: Um no. No, thank you. Never ever. Not if he were the last human being on Earth.

@HannahLaRosa: Yeah, Brandon's tough. I think there's a soft heart under the gruff exterior, but he's definitely an acquired taste.

@Andi: Didn't you say he kidnapped you?

I generally don't want to know anything about Brandon Nix, but I am admittedly dying to know that story.

@HannahLaRosa: Long story. But I'm sure that's not why you reached out. What's going on? Why does my following matter?

Right. I need to stay focused. This situation is bad, and it's only bound to get worse if I can't nip it in the bud. The feeling of desperation overwhelms me, and I type out the whole sob story about Nathan threatening my job. But as soon as I hit send, regret consumes me.

What did I just do? I don't know Hannah LaRosa, other than what I see on social media. I don't know the type of person she is. I don't know that she won't write a tell-all story, putting her own spin on it. If she does, I'll never officiate another soccer game.

Chances are my career is already over either way.

I stare at the messages in the ClikClak app, wishing I could have a re-do over the last day. If Brandon hadn't made me pose with that kid. If Brandon hadn't said hi to Mike. If the plane hadn't made an emergency landing. If Brandon hadn't squeezed my hand so tightly. If that baby hadn't had a tantrum. If Benj had only told me he wasn't in Denver, I never would have been on that plane to begin with. If Brandon hadn't screamed in my face in the first place, I wouldn't have felt the need to run away to the safety of my brother.

It all circles back to Brandon Nix.

I truly do hate that man.

CHAPTER 14: BRANDON

Once I get to Wyoming, I find out very quickly why Jess isn't responsive to my text messages. She lives literally in the middle of nowhere and gets no cell reception.

It's nice to unplug, actually.

What's nicer is seeing my sister happy and healthy. She's an honest-to-God cowgirl. She repairs fences and herds cattle and sheep. She feeds and waters them and rides a horse and owns cowboy boots in an unironic way.

This is the best I've seen her since before the accident.

As we sit around a legit campfire, we talk about it for the first time in years.

"I let the accident define me for too long. It was a tragedy, but it happened to me. It isn't me. It isn't who I am."

Her words hover in the air, floating away with the sparks and embers the fire spits out into the inky black night. I've heard encouraging words from her before. I've believed her before. I'm not going to be duped again.

"That's great, Jess, but what happens the next time something bad happens? How are you going to deal with it?"

She shrugs, holding my gaze. That is something different. When she's using, she avoids eye contact. Now her amber eyes are bright and clear. She couldn't fake that. We'll see how long it lasts.

We're up at the ass-crack of dawn because it turns out ranchers really do get up with the sun. I make the drive back to Jackson Hole and return the truck I rented. Once again, I'm running late and barely make it before my flight takes off. I barely have time to doze off before we're touching down in Denver where I change planes. I finally turn my phone back on.

Holy shit.

I'm viral.

That's pretty cool.

Except all of ClikClak is speculating whether I'm involved with Andi Nichols.

Not if she were the last woman on Earth.

Not only is she not my type, but she's also one of the most unfriendly human beings ever. It's as if just standing in my presence taxes her. Whatever. I don't know what I ever did to her to justify her attitude.

Lots of soccer players yell at refs. Other than being overly dramatic with injuries, it's what we're known for. I wasn't going to back down simply because she has lady bits. If she wants to ref in the men's league, then she needs to be prepared to accept how refs there get treated.

It wouldn't be pro soccer without some dramatics. We've got to keep the people entertained somehow. Soccer simply doesn't have the excitement that football does. Sure, it's infinitely more athletic—you won't see any pro soccer players with beer guts—but ninety minutes with only a few scoring occasions can make the crowd lose interest.

Plus, we're just drama junkies.

I scroll through ClikClak some more while waiting for my next flight. It's only then that I notice the text message from my dad.

Dad: CALL ME

I don't know if he knows that it's considered shouty caps, but it's a moot point. Every communication we have is shouty caps, at least in the vibe if not the actual font.

"Hey, Dad, I just got your message. I'm on my way back from seeing Jess in Wy—"

"What are you thinking leaving mid-season like this? You should be training if you're not playing."

"It was three days. I went to see Jess to—"

"It didn't look like you were going to see her. It looked like you were sneaking off with Andi Nichols. Do you know what this could do for your reputation, damaged as it already is?"

"I wasn't sneaking off with her. Hell, I didn't even know she was sitting next to me until I woke up." Now that I think of it, how did she get into that seat?

Dad's voice rises. "Jesus, Brandon, you sat with her? Are you a special kind of stupid or something? Maybe you've taken one too many soccer balls to the head."

With that kind of support from my parent-slash-manager, who needs haters?

"I got on a plane. There was an empty seat next to me. I fell asleep. I woke up while the plane was hitting massive turbulence, forcing us to make an emergency landing. She was in the seat next to me. We had a brief stop at the smallest airport in the world, and then we got back on the plane and flew to Denver. I slept most of the way. That's it. What do you want me to say?"

"Why don't you ever think? If people think you're in a relationship with her, people are going to think you're a cheater. The Buzzards are this close to letting you go because of all your other problems. They let me know you're on probation. And no matter how good I am at wheeling and dealing, I won't be able to convince any team to take someone with an attitude issue who also cheats by sleeping with the officials."

"So where should I mail your 'Number One Fan' merch to since you're obviously the president of the Brandon Nix Fan Club?" Without waiting for an answer, I hang up.

My relationship with my dad is complicated. I wish I could say it wasn't always like this, but it's hard to remember a time when it wasn't. Intense is a good word to describe him. Intense and unforgiving.

Those words would be perfect on his gravestone.

I'm sure people who know him now think that the accident that killed my mom changed my dad, but he was always an asshole. He's just a bigger one now.

He doesn't even like soccer. He never has.

But he certainly likes having a professional athlete for a son who makes a nice fat salary that he can collect a commission from. My dad's not nearly as good at managing me as he thinks he is. If he were, I'd have some nice brand endorsement deals, like the one Callaghan Entay just landed.

Entay's one lucky bastard. His life is perfect.

My life will never be that way. It wasn't from the beginning. It doesn't matter if I play by the rules and walk the straight and narrow. I'm always going to get the short end of the stick.

My dad's the world's biggest douchecanoe. My mom was killed in a car accident when I was 18. I don't even like soccer that much. I just happen to be insanely good at it. I'm not bragging—it's the truth. That's a curse in and of itself. The world thinks you have to do it because you're innately talented. No one would let me quit, even if I tried.

When I tried.

That's when I got massively guilt-tripped into staying and playing. And now what? I'm 32 years old. I'm one of the best at what I do, but no one likes me. Who cares about that? I own that. I'm an asshole.

But to insinuate that I'm cheating and sleeping with a ref to do it, that's just bullshit.

I'm a lot of things, but a cheater isn't one of them.

And while part of me might be relieved at the idea of not being able to play soccer anymore, I have nothing else in my life. Without soccer, I'm nothing with no one. I may not like it, but I need soccer.

I can't lose the only thing I have.

CHAPTER 15: ANDI

Han Solo said it best with the immortal words, "I've got a bad feeling about this." It runs through my head on repeat as I read back the text chain with Hannah LaRosa. We moved off of messaging on ClikClak and onto regular texting as the plans developed.

I should trust her judgment. She's built her career on working the algorithm, and it's landed her a job managing social media for the Patriots. As last we left it, she was going to do some research and see if she could come up with some social media strategies that might help mitigate damage to my career.

I've got to get out in front of this quickly. I haven't heard from Nathan yet, but it's only a matter of time. Every time my phone pings I want to jump out of my skin. But it's quiet.

Too quiet.

I have games I'm scheduled to officiate over the weekend, so I'll have to be in contact with the USSLRA office then. I'm dreading it. If only I knew what Hannah was going to come up with, so I had some damage control in place before that, maybe I'd sleep a little easier.

Since I'm so restless, I do the next best thing. I go for a run. I'm one of the few people out on this steamy July day, but I consider it good training. Soccer games are never called on account of the weather being too hot. I've got to be able to run up and down the field with the players for the full duration of the game.

The only way to do that is to train like a player. It's one of the main criticisms for having female referees in the MUSSL, to begin with—that they won't be able to keep up with the pace of the game.

I'd rather drop dead from heatstroke than prove them right.

I mean, not really. Heatstroke totally sucks and makes you feel downright shitty. You have to be smart when you're working out in this kind of weather.

There's a decent chance that I'm not being smart because I'm letting my emotions take over. I deliberately slow my pace and try to even my breathing. God, it's hot out here.

I'm barely walking when I finally get back to my place. The air conditioner can't keep up with the thick humidity of the day, so I open up my freezer and stand there until my sweat-soaked skin is covered in goosebumps.

Knowing I'll regret it tomorrow, I skip my post-run stretch in lieu of a lukewarm shower. I stand there for way too long, trying to make my mind stop racing.

Prior to last week, my goal had been to work twenty more games this season so I could be promoted to the next level. With the bump in salary as a Level 2, in addition to my savings, I'd be able to quit my day job. I could probably do some part-time, off-season consulting work to make sure I have a nest egg for unplanned occurrences. I might have to make some thoughtful choices here and there, but I could do it.

Once you get to Level 2, USSLRA also provides health insurance. That's a biggie too. The biggie. These are the glamorous things you get to think about when you're an adult that no one talks about when you're a bright-eyed, idealistic youngster.

Of course, with Benj, health insurance has always been a hot topic in our house. Then, when I worked in the clinic as a physical therapist, I had to document to justify why my services were needed. In other words, every day I had to prove my worth. As shitty as that is, somehow it's better than my current soul-sucking job.

I hate making therapists prove that their patients need this equipment. I know they do. No one *wants* to have a special toileting system or a wheelchair. I love refereeing, but I do my job to pay the bills.

I'd really prefer if the job I loved could also keep a roof over my head and food on my table.

I won't be able to referee forever. My days on the pitch are limited, so I need to strike while the iron's hot. Or grab the bull by the horns. Or some other super clichéd motivational crap.

I don't know what spin-doctoring Hannah LaRosa is going to come up with, but I hope it's good. We haven't talked about fees yet, so I hope I can afford her services. I'm probably too trusting, but she doesn't seem like the type to rip me off.

I cannot begin to fathom what she's going to come up with for me to do. I hope it's not lip-synching or dancing on ClikClak. I don't think I could make a fool of myself like that simply for entertainment. Maybe I could do videos teaching about the rules of soccer.

I bet there are a lot of people who would be interested in something like that. Especially with soccer gaining more popularity here in the U.S. That would be a cool thing to do.

I hope that's part of Hannah's plan.

After my shower, I throw on a tank top and some running shorts and sit down at my computer to attempt to catch up on some work. That's when I see it.

The email from Nathan.

They want me to come in for a Monday morning meeting following my WUSSL game in Birmingham on Saturday. The USSLRA headquarters are in Atlanta, so it makes sense while I'm in that zone of the country. They don't want to pay to fly me there twice.

Which makes sense if they're going to fire me.

The knot squeezes tight in my stomach as a wave of nausea passes over me. Whatever Hannah's coming up with, it needs to be fast.

And good.

The inner me wants to pace around my apartment and hyperventilate and throw things. The outer me, even though I'm alone, does my best to keep cool, calm, and collected. I sit lotus style on my couch and attempt to meditate.

I don't have the time or energy to waste *feeling*. I need to be doing. That's what my mom always did. She didn't sit around bemoaning the fact that her son was born with a form of muscular dystrophy. Nope, she threw herself into it. She learned everything she could—and this was before the internet—which meant a lot of trips to the library and copying articles from microfiche. Kids today will never know how good they have it.

Then, there was the fundraising. We even got to fly to Las Vegas to be on Jerry Lewis's MDA Labor Day Telethon when Benj was about five. I swear, if my mom wasn't taking Benj to therapy, she was fundraising. And her efforts worked.

I mean, maybe not her directly, but as part of the larger collective. There have been new—

I jump to my feet. That's it! Fundraising!

That's what I need. A cause. A worthy cause. There's only one in my book, but I'll get involved again. I'll take it public and that can be my platform. I owe it to the community. Without the recent gene therapies and medical advances, Benj wouldn't still be here. When he was diagnosed, his life expectancy was *maybe* 30 at best. He's 32 now and obviously doing well enough to go gallivanting across the country.

I quickly dash off a message to Hannah with this idea. It's time for me to give back, and if it helps clear my name and reputation at the same time, then it's a win-win all the way around.

Just how I like it.

CHAPTER 16: BRANDON

I expect a little flak from Coach Janssen or the rest of the team about my sudden vacation, but no one says anything to me. It's like they didn't even notice I wasn't there.

Maybe they're already convinced I'm getting fired.

My dad's going to have a field day with this one.

Today, everyone is focused on Callaghan Entay and his return from the Global Games. While the U.S. National Team did better than predicted, they lost in the round of 8. As I walk by Entay, I say, "If I'd been on the National Team, we'd probably have made it to the semifinals."

I don't know why I say it, other than no one is paying attention to me. It's as if I'm made of glass and they can see right through me.

Entay doesn't look up from tying his cleats when he retorts, "So you could blow it by getting a penalty in the box and then whiffing your shot in the kickoff?"

Touché.

I'm about to let it slide when Landon Stubbs breaks out in a guffaw. "Ooh, he got you, didn't he?"

Andy Bracer chimes in. "It's totally your fault we lost in the semifinals last year. You should have been fined. Or fired." Andy plays left wing. There are midfielders who score more than he does.

Suddenly I'm the center of attention, but this isn't the type of attention I want. I snap, "Samson missed his PK too. Go give him some shit."

It's true. In the semifinals for the USSL National Championship last year, it was a one-one tie after regulation play. We went into overtime and neither team scored, so it was onto the penalty kicks. Both Pressley Samson and I missed ours. Callaghan Entay only stopped one of five shots the Miami Wave had.

It's just as much their fault as it is mine.

But I get the blame. Story of my life.

There's no more squabbling as it's time to get to work. As practice winds down, I see Callaghan approaching. I'm not in the mood for more shit and more finger-pointing. "Can I talk to you a minute?" His tone is serious.

Great. Callaghan's also the captain, which means I'm probably going to be censured or benched or fined or some other bullshit. I take a deep breath in, ready to defend myself, when Callaghan starts. "Okay, this is weird, but my girlfriend asked me to talk to you." Callaghan looks at his feet, running his hand through his sweat-soaked hair.

There's only one thing I can think of that would make a dude this uncomfortable. I hold up my hands.

"Listen man, I'm flattered and all, but I'm not gonna have a threesome with a teammate, I don't care how much his lady wants me. You don't shit where you eat. You should probably remember that." I cock my head. "You know, I didn't think Hannah was the type to be into that.

Entay's head whips up. "No, Jesus, no. That's not what I was talking about at all." A shudder runs through his body. It almost looks as if he chokes back a gag. "Anyway, as I was saying, Hannah asked me to set up a meeting with you. She does social media stuff, and she had an idea to help improve your image and all."

I cock my head to the side. Now there's a thought. Maybe if she could make me look better online, they'll take me off probation here. "Is she any good at it?"

He shrugs. "Not sure if anyone is good enough to help you. You're your own worst enemy."

"I am not. I'm fine. Other people just can't handle my level of honesty. Those are the people with something to hide."

"Those are the people with an internal filter. You should think about getting one."

"Can I buy it on Amazon?"

Entay shakes his head, turning away. "I'm going to text you the information. Just show up, shut up, and try to not stick your foot in your mouth for a few minutes. She might be able to help you, and from how the front office is talking, you need all the help you can get right about now."

Fuck, he's right.

Entay does know his shit on and off the field. I look up his girlfriend on ClikClak. She's got an impressive following. Her bio reads: Sports Analyst, New England Patriots Social Media Manager, Funny Dog Parody Videos.

Maybe it wouldn't hurt to at least talk to her.

Her dog videos are pretty funny, so at least she's upfront and honest about that. Something doesn't sit right with me though. Why does she want to meet with me? I mean, shouldn't I be seeking her out, not the other way around?

I'll go in with my guard up. That's the standard resting position for me anyway. Living my life with the family I have—you only get hurt by opening up. It may be one reason why I'm so honest and blunt. I know people can't handle me right away, instead of investing time and energy only to be deserted.

Entay texts me the name of a restaurant, along with the time. I google it only to find out the place is in Charlestown. Shit, that's a hike.

I text him back.

> *Me: Why we gotta go all the way up there?*
> *Entay: Why you gotta question everything? Just be there. Or don't. It's not my career on the line*

When he puts it that way ...

It takes me almost an hour to drive there. This had better be worth it. It's right by The Garden, so parking is a pain. They don't even have valet. I don't have a good feeling about this. I mean, the place looks okay. It looks like the type of place I would pick—if it were in my neighborhood. I bet they have good steaks. The late-July night has cooled down enough that sitting outside would be nice.

I see Callaghan waiting at the host station. "We should grab a table outside." I nod my head toward the brick patio.

He shakes his head. "We're this way."

"Come on, man. It's nice and there are tables out there."

Entay stops. "Jesus, Nix, can't you do anything without an argument?"

I hold up my hands. "No need to get your panties in a wad. It just looked nice out there. It's not a big deal. You don't need to overreact."

I get this sort of thing a lot. People expect me to fly off the handle or fight them, so they fight first. Maybe ... *just maybe* ... this is something I should bring up to Watson Ross. Like, why are people always picking a fight with me, when I haven't even done anything?

It's obviously a them problem.

Still, he should be able to teach me a magic saying, like "slow your roll" or something to keep people from being wound too tightly around me.

I follow Entay through the restaurant to a back room. Where the restaurant itself is dark wood, polished tile, black accents, and cast in a red hue from the awnings that overhang all the windows, this room looks like something out of a dollhouse. The wood is lighter. There are greens and pinks and flowers.

Yuck.

And then I see Andi Nichols sitting at a back corner booth with Hannah LaRosa. Double yuck.

For Andi, not Hannah. I don't have a reason to think that way about Hannah yet, but I have a feeling I'll get there soon enough. After all, we're in a storybook setting, and she brought a person who hates me.

This is not going to go well.

CHAPTER 17: ANDI

The moment Brandon Nix walks in, I want to run out. This is not a good idea, and it's not going to work. I don't know what I was thinking. I grip the edge to prevent myself from vaulting over the table and sprinting for the door.

It's odd to see him outside of workout clothes or his soccer uniform. Jeans and a faded red T-shirt. Red hair tie on his wrist. Those same flip-flops he wore on the plane. Does he own anything besides these and his soccer cleats? His hair is down, with waves and curls most women would sell their souls to have, despite the bad bleach job that is growing out. Trimming about five inches off would do him wonders. He's wearing black-rimmed glasses, which totally changes his look.

For the better, that is.

I'm not sure I would have recognized him. Until he speaks, of course.

"Hello, Andrew."

That's it. I'm outta here. I'll take out a full-page ad in *The Looking Glass* if I have to. I'm not doing this. I stand up. "This is stupid. It will never work. Hannah, I'm sorry I wasted your time."

Brandon Nix holds up his hands. "What about me? I drove all the way up here. Do you know what traffic is like this time of day? I think you owe me an apology, Andrew. Or at least a steak."

I grind my teeth together. "Stop calling me Andrew. My name is Andi."

He shrugs. "Potato, pah-tah-toe."

Hannah stands up, completing our Mexican standoff. We stare at each other for a long moment. Finally, she says, "Guys, this is not going to work if you're going to act like children. My babysitting days are long done, now sit down."

Slowly, without breaking his gaze, I sink back onto the upholstered bench. Brandon sits down casually like he doesn't have a care in the world—like his career isn't on the line—and flags the waitress over. He orders a double whiskey, neat. We continue to stare at each other until the waitress returns. Still without breaking eye contact, he picks up his glass tumbler and drains the amber liquid. He puts the glass down and slowly drags the back of his hand across his mouth.

I cave. "You know that's why they invented napkins." I pick up the piece of cloth from the table and toss it at him. I swear, it's as if he's never been out in public before.

"Okay, well, this has been fun, but let's put the childish games aside, put our grown-up panties on, and get to work." Hannah pulls out a folder and begins riffling through papers. "As best I can see it, the both of you have an image problem. That's the common ground."

Brandon looks at Hannah and then me, surprise in his eyes. "What's your problem? I mean, aside from the obvious stick up your ass?"

I sigh. "Thanks to your antics during the Buzzards–Terrors game, the viral video clips have inspired the internet to ship us." I look at Hannah. "Did I say it right?"

She laughs. "For the most part."

I continue. "I'm not sure if you're aware, but the USSLRA is an ole boys' club. They don't take too kindly to us womenfolk showing that we're capable. It's why I was the first ever woman to be the head official in a MUSSL game."

Brandon stops me. "MUSSL? What's that?"

If I sighed every time he exasperated me, I'd be hyperventilating. Instead, I give him my best bored expression and womansplain it to him. "Well, you have the United States Soccer League. The USSL. Under that, you have two divisions. The *Men's* United States Soccer League and the *Women's* United States Soccer League. The MUSSL and the WUSSL."

He laughs. "Sounds like muscle and wuscle. Or wuss. Like for the strong men and the wimpy wo—" He stops mid-sentence. "Oh. Is that what you mean by the ole boys' club?"

I raise my eyebrows, completely shocked that he got it. I thought I'd need a whiteboard and marker to spell it out for him. "Yes. And when referring to the men's league as the USSL, you're making that the default and automatically making the women less or second-class."

Brandon doesn't come back with a smart-ass reply. I pull out my phone to check the weather app to see if Hell has frozen over.

Nope. That's weird.

It's almost as if Brandon and I might see eye to eye on something.

Hannah says, "And Brandon, you're on thin ice with the Buzzards. They're not going to deal with much more from you, on or off the pitch. There's an incredible wealth of young talent in the minor leagues chomping at the bit. Pro-teams in the MUSSL aren't going to put the energy—or the money—into someone who's a P.R. disaster."

He shrugs. "I can always go play in the British Football League. That's the upper tier anyway."

Hannah levels her gaze at him. "Edmund Jones will not put up with it either. Think of how he treated Xavier Henry."

If I'm not mistaken, Brandon pales slightly. Xavier was big news this past winter. He'd been expelled a few years back from the BFL after a situation with Edmund Jones's daughter. Turns out, Xavier did nothing wrong, and she set him up. Even though his name has been cleared, he's still on a lifetime ban from the BFL.

We all know the BFL isn't a viable option for Brandon.

"So why are we here? It's not like Andrew is running for president of the Brandon Nix Fan Club," he grumbles.

Hannah sighs. "No, Andi is not."

Brandon sits back with a smug smile on his face. "So if she's not going to be a Nixen, what does Andi need from me? I'll ask again. Why are we here?" He cocks an eyebrow under the black frame, his dark brown eyes twinkling.

If I didn't know any better, I'd think he was enjoying this.

I open my mouth to speak, but Hannah starts first. We'd agreed ahead of time that she should probably do most of the talking, knowing that Brandon would oppose anything I said simply out of spite. "You need a P.R. makeover, ASAP. Andi needs to quiet any rumors or speculation that she's acting with impropriety with any players in the league. And the fact that you two were seen this past week flying to Denver together doesn't help either of you."

I fold my hands on the table and wait. This idea had seemed good when we'd talked about it yesterday. In fact, Hannah was super excited when I called her with my idea.

Hannah continues. "We need a reason why you were both on that flight together that isn't a romantic rendezvous."

I suppress a shudder when she says that.

"Andi suggested that you two announce and put together a charity initiative. That way there's a reason you were going to Denver."

"I wasn't even going to Denver. I went to Wyoming. Denver was just a stop on the way to Jackson Hole. Or wherever the hell in the middle of nowhere I went once the plane landed. I don't even know. All I know is I didn't get cell reception and cows really do smell like farts."

Nice.

I glance at Hannah who looks like she's biting her tongue. Literally. Her jaw is clenched so tightly I'm afraid she's going to break a tooth. She stands. "I'm going out to the main restaurant to get a drink. Or ten. I suggest that the two of you find some common ground so we can get your charitable acts in motion. Otherwise, both your careers are probably dead in the water."

She leaves and I take a sip of my gin and tonic. There's nothing like it in the summer. I look at Brandon Nix and immediately drain the rest of my drink. I flag the server down to order another, and Brandon gestures for himself as well.

"Surely we can find some common ground," I finally say. "We're both adults here. There has to be something we can agree would be a worthy cause to lend our names to."

Brandon scoffs. "I doubt you and I have anything in common."

I start with the lowest hanging fruit. "We both like soccer."

His head tilts slightly, but he doesn't say anything. It doesn't matter, it's a tell. Remind me to challenge him in poker someday. I'd be sure to clean house with him as an opponent.

"Why don't you want to do something with soccer?"

"I didn't say that." His eyes dart around the room, looking at everything but me.

A-ha! Got him. "You didn't have to. It's written all over your face."

Still, he doesn't say anything. Alrighty then. I try another approach. "A ranch in Wyoming? What were you doing out there?"

"Visiting my sister." His voice is gruff and guarded. Not like the Brandon Nix I so often see.

"Funny, I was on my way to visit my brother. I hope your visit went better than mine."

His gaze shifts to mine immediately. "What happened?"

"My brother wasn't there. I landed in Denver and immediately flew back to Boston the same day. It was the longest day ever." I order another drink.

"What do you mean he wasn't there? Why would you go see him if he wasn't in Denver? I'm so confused."

"I had no reason to believe he wouldn't be there. Except ..." I don't know how to say that Benj didn't tell me. Didn't think I was important enough to tell. "Anyway, there was a miscommunication, and I didn't get to see him after all."

It's lame, but it's not as if I'm going to tell Brandon Nix all about my life. We're here to figure out what charity we're going to work with, and that's it.

This is just about saving my career.

CHAPTER 18: BRANDON

Talking to Andi Nichols is like watching paint dry. No, that's not it. She's boring. Nope, that's not it either. I try to put my finger on it. She's totally closed off.

Why?

She has no expression on her face. Yet the lack of expression in a way is an expression. Every so often, it seems like something peeks through, but then she shuts it down. What's she hiding?

Now it's a side quest to find out what's underneath, which is actually pretty interesting. I'm seeing her through a new lens. I'm not sure if she tries to hide from everyone or just me. But that piques my curiosity. I have to know. There's something ... I can't put my finger on it.

Maybe she's a secret government agent. Traveling around for soccer games would be the perfect cover.

Like why would she fly all the way to Denver to see someone who wasn't there? Wouldn't she tell them she was coming? Who just decides to drop in on someone from three time zones away?

Or two. I don't remember how far Denver is. The time zone thing always messes me up anyway.

"So, what were you doing on a cattle ranch? How did your flip-flops make out there?"

I glance down at my feet. I couldn't tell you what I was wearing, but she knew. Interesting. She notices details. That's one tally for the "Andrew is a secret spy" column.

For the record, flip-flops do not go well on the ranch. I had to borrow a too-small pair of boots while I was there. Jess got a big kick out of that one. She even texted me a picture. I think she's going to use it to extort money out of me someday. Maybe sell it to *The Looking Glass* or something.

"I was visiting my sister."

"So in all honesty, we were both going to visit our siblings," Andi says. "I wish that could be it. That we didn't have to make up something else. Why can't the truth be good enough?"

"Your brother wasn't in Denver though? What happened there? How did you not know?" I still can't figure that one out.

"You don't know where in Wyoming your sister lives. How do you not know?"

Good comeback. Also, she's answering a question with a question. I've seen enough thriller movies to know that's a classic spy interrogation technique. "She just moved there."

"Oh, so you're not from Wyoming? Where are you from?"

Great. We're going to do this. Cue the sympathy violins. "I grew up in Upstate New York, outside of Albany. But there's no pro or semi-pro team there, so I started moving around a lot by the time I was in middle school."

"Where's the rest of your family?"

Here we go.

"My dad lives in North Jersey. My sister's in Wyoming now. My mom's dead." I like to go for the shock value on that. It keeps people from asking questions I don't want to talk about. When I put it like that, I get the uncomfortable "I'm sorries" and then people change the subject as quickly as possible.

She doesn't placate me with pity. "Yeah, it can be tough. My brother has a terminal illness, so he's been on a death watch his entire life. It's why I was surprised he wasn't there. Apparently, his new medication has not only added years to his life, but life to his years. He and his girlfriend are road-tripping."

That was probably the last thing I expected to hear from Andi Nichols. She's full of surprises.

"Okay, so we each have a sibling," I offer. The sooner we find our common ground, the sooner we can figure this out and go.

She drains another drink almost as soon as the waitress puts it down. Good idea. I order another. I'm going to regret this in the morning, and I have no idea how I'm going to get home. If Callaghan gives me shit at practice for being hungover, I'll put the blame squarely on him—where it belongs. Speaking of which ... "Do you think Hannah and Callaghan are still here? Are they holding us hostage? Are they going to pick up the bill for tonight?"

Andi's eyebrows scrunch together. "Why would they be picking up the bill? They were doing us a favor, arranging this meeting. I doubted you would come if I'd asked you directly, and we needed to be discreet. We can't have anyone think we're sneaking around. That's why we're in the room back here."

Does she not see the irony in this plan? "Isn't that exactly what we're doing? There's no one else in this room but us."

"No, we need to have a legit plan." She keeps talking. "So my brother has a genetic disease called Spinal Muscular Atrophy. It's in the Muscular Dystrophy family. I'm always happy to do something for that. Of course, I'd also be happy to do some sort of fundraiser for women in sports. Those are some causes near and dear to my heart." Now she takes a long sip from her water. "I just want it to be something important. You know, something that matters."

I think about a cause near and dear to my own heart; the only thing that matters to me right now. "What about drug addiction? Keeping kids clean and all."

Andi rolls her eyes, her mask cracking wide open. "Are you kidding me?" she slurs. "That's so overdone. Plus, when are people going to start taking accountability for themselves? No one makes them do the drungs." She looks surprised and tries again.

"Drungs. Druuuuugs." She nods triumphantly. "My brother didn't get a choice about being born with a disease that will kill him. An addict isn't born one."

That's it. I don't want to listen anymore.

I push my chair away from the table. "This isn't going to work. I don't think we'd even be able to agree on anything. And you're totally wrong about drug addiction. It's a disease, just like your brother's. But because of narrow-minded people like you, all it gets is shame. Do you know how hard it is to recover when the world judges you for having a disease?"

I throw a few hundred dollars on the table—even though we never got around to eating—and storm out. I cannot be in the same room with that woman. I'd rather never play soccer again.

And she deserves to lose her career.

Entay chases me out onto the street. Where the hell am I? I try to get my bearings. I'm close to the Zakim Bridge. Where did I park my car? It's in a garage somewhere. Fuck, I'm too far from home to Uber.

"I can't drive."

Entay shakes his head. "No, you can't. I thought I was going to have to wrestle the keys away from you."

What? I run my fingers through my hair, scraping it back into a low ponytail. "Fuuuck, you think I'm that bad?"

Even in my whiskey-soaked brain, I know this is bad. If my own team captain thinks I'm horrible enough to drink and drive, then I am truly alone in this fight. No one believes in me.

I see Andi also stumble out, Hannah by her side. I point my finger at her. "This is your fault. And now everyone thinks I'm the scum of the Earth." I turn my menacing finger on Entay. "I hate you all."

I start to walk down the street. There's got to be a hotel around here somewhere. I'm used to not being liked. I don't need to be liked. I am good at what I do and that's all that should matter. But somehow— right now—it's not enough.

"Brandon, wait up!"

I stop. Of the three people I walked away from, she's the last one I'd expect to chase me down. "What is it, Andrew? Am I going to get another lecture about how addiction is a choice, not a *real* disease? Any other soapboxes you want to get up on? Or do you just like kicking a man where it hurts?"

She looks stunned at my tirade. Then she blinks and starts speaking, a slight slur edging her words. "We have to come up with something. Don't you understand? I'm desperate," she pants. Odd because I've seen her run up and down the soccer field and barely break a sweat.

I lean in and sniff the area where her jaw meets her ear. "Oh, I can tell. I can smell it wafting off of you." Not a particularly kind thing to say, but I'm not feeling in a particularly kind mood.

And it's a lie. She smells like lavender and citrus.

She puts her hand on my arm, trying to stop me from leaving. "Listen, I wouldn't be here if I had any other choices. The only person who can offer an alternate explanation as to why we were together is you."

"Have you thought about the truth?"

Andi pulls her hand back as if I were a hot stove. Bitterly she says, "I live in a world where the truth doesn't matter. The only thing that matters is how it's perceived. And once someone has made up their mind, nothing will change it."

She walks away, and I'm left standing there on the street for a moment before I hail a cab to take me to the nearest hotel. Her words ricochet in my head, interrupting my sleep.

No one interrupts my sleep.

Certainly not some pain-in-the-ass referee who has it out for me but then puts the salvation of both our careers in our collective hands.

Both our careers.

Fuck, I know she's right. If my own teammates think I'm the kind of scum who would get behind a wheel drunk, well, that says it all, doesn't it? I'm a blowhard. I'm a loudmouth. I'm a womanizer. I don't have an internal filter.

But I'd never take someone's mom from them. I'd never leave a poor sixteen-year-old kid so wracked with guilt that she becomes an addict. I can't have the public thinking that of me. I may not be a lot, but I'm not that guy.

Shit, I'm going to have to go along with this stupid plan.

CHAPTER 19: ANDI

When my phone lights up showing Hannah LaRosa is calling, my first instinct is to throw the phone out the window. There's nothing she can say to reverse the disaster that last night was.

Especially not after a picture surfaced on Instagram, followed by multiple videos with that picture showing the four of us outside Prima. In reality, Brandon and I were snapping at each other.

Have I mentioned I hate that man?

But in the picture, all you see is his body, bent toward mine, his nose inches from my ear.

If I didn't know better, I'd think it was an intimate moment, not him telling me I smelled desperate.

More fuel to the bonfire that was my career.

I leave in two days for Birmingham and then have the meeting with Nathan two days after that. Unless I can come up with something good, there's no reason why I'd be with two players from the Boston Buzzards on what looked like a double date.

"Yes, I saw. I know it's bad." I don't even bother saying hello. "But that oaf won't even sit down for a civilized conversation, so what can I do?"

"He wants you to come down to his place to talk. He doesn't want to be out in public."

"I'm supposed to work today. I travel this week, so I have to get five days of work done in two. Plus, I still need to get a run in. I'm trying to wait until it cools down a little."

Hannah laughs. "That's something I do not miss about playing soccer. If I want to work out, I do. For the record, I never want to."

"There are definitely days I want to skip it, but God forbid I can't keep up. It took me this long to get in the door. I don't need to give them an excuse to kick me out." I pause a moment. "Another excuse, that is. Though I'm a little pissed at the straws they're currently grasping at."

Hannah says, "It's hard to fight for your place in a world that sees you as lesser simply because you're female. I know. I applied for an awful lot of sportscaster jobs. They couldn't come right out and tell me they wouldn't hire me because I'm a woman. They did feel free to use my weight—sorry, my *image*—as an excuse. I can't wrap my mind around how we live in a society that doesn't think women have a place in sports."

"Yeah, I know. It doesn't make a whole lot of sense, but it's what's going on. I'm probably going to reach out to my union. I haven't done anything wrong, but they are making me feel like I have."

"I've never had a union, but that might be a good place to start."

I don't really do much with my union, other than pay dues. Maybe it's time to put those dues to good use. "Still, I need to do some damage control on my end. You know, cover my ass a little. If I can do that first, then I'll reach out to the union." I think about my upcoming meeting in Atlanta. I don't have a lot of time to lose. If Brandon wants to talk, maybe I should listen. "Fine. I'll drive down. Text me his address."

I work without stopping for lunch, trying to crank out as many cases as I can. I have strict rubrics and guidelines to follow about what I can approve and what I have to deny. I try to be as absolutely lenient as I can, especially when the request has followed all the requirements for submission.

You'd be surprised how many people submit a claim that doesn't have the basic information required. Those are automatic denials or requests for further information. I have about twelve of those today. Normally that would frustrate me, but today it just makes me look super productive.

I don't need to give my other job an excuse to fire me too.

I'm wearing short running shorts and a tank top. I don't feel like changing, so I don't. I don't think the paparazzi are staking me out, but if they were, they'd be hard pressed to spin my attire and appearance as date-worthy. I'm definitely not trying to impress Brandon Nix. The only thing that separates my appearance from my normal gym look is that my hair is down. I washed it this morning, and for some reason, I actually blow-dried it rather than slicking it back into its normal ponytail or braid. I don't usually put any effort into my hair. I'm not sure what possessed me to do it today.

But damn if it didn't actually come out pretty. Maybe I should do this more often?

I plug Brandon's address into my phone. Geez, now I realize why he was complaining about driving to the restaurant in Charlestown last night. It's a hike and a half, and there's no easy way to get to his house. I'm stuck in rush-hour traffic with the masses leaving the city and heading to their homes in the suburbs. I could never do this kind of commute.

I live just outside the northwestern city limits in Everett. It's close enough to be able to get to the airport for my flights out, but I can still have a car for when I need to drive. Plus, it's cheaper than living in Boston proper. Brandon lives all the way down in Walpole.

On the drive down I-93, I try to picture what Brandon's house will look like. He's got a flashy car. A Porsche something. I'm sure his house has lots of shiny, white marble floors. It's definitely going to be on the gaudy side, that's for certain.

I bet he has statues of nude women.

I am so not prepared for what I see when I pull into the driveway at the address my phone has directed me to. It's a midcentury cedar wood A-frame. It's smaller than I imagined. Hell, it's nothing like I would have possibly pictured Brandon Nix calling home. There's a large brick chimney that goes up the center of the building. I would not call it aesthetically pleasing. I'm so disoriented by the appearance of the house that I forget to be apprehensive.

I walk to the front door and knock. Brandon pulls the door open. He appears to be fresh off a workout, complete with a legit 1980s terrycloth sweatband holding his locks off his forehead. He looks stupid. I focus on that, rather than the fact that he's wearing gym shorts, a sheen of sweat, and nothing else. Yup, that's one mighty stupid-looking sweatband.

I may not like him, but I have eyes. And a pulse. And a sex drive.

Also, I think I thought he'd be covered in tattoos. I don't see any on his arms … or chest … or back.

Interesting.

"Andrew," he greets. And that's all it takes. His voice is akin to a bucket of ice-cold water dumped over my head. Time to focus on something else.

I look over his shoulder to see what his house looks like. This place is so unexpected. There's oak everywhere. Doors, trim, cabinets, beams. What's not wood is glass. Just from where I'm standing in the living room, I count at least three sliding glass doors. There's a large room to the side that is a home gym, and off of that is a glass-enclosed three-season room.

The reason for the glass soon becomes clear. The house is on a lake, nestled in a grove of tall pine trees. I saw another house driving in that seems pretty similar—like they were on a lot that was subdivided or something—but from inside the house, all you see is the water.

It's gorgeous.

The view, not the house. The house looks like something my grandmother decorated.

"This is not how I pictured you living." I don't know why I say it. It seems like a very Brandon thing to say. "This view is amazing though." I walk up to one of the glass doors to get a better look.

Brandon stands next to me, also gazing at the water. "I couldn't resist. I didn't know I wanted something by water, but the minute I saw it, I knew I needed it."

I nod, nothing else to say. I would feel the same way. It's July, so the days are long. Sunset is a few hours away, and several kayakers are taking advantage out on the water. It must be nice to live a life of leisure that affords you time to kayak after work.

"You hit a nerve last night. You all did. It's why I acted the way I did," he says, his voice low.

I turn, startled by his admission. Also a little startled because I'd gotten so lost in my reverie about the lake, I forgot he was standing next to me. "Your behavior was about what I expected. I didn't see anything unusual."

His brow tightens into a frown. "Whatever. I'm going to take a quick shower. I'll be right back."

He disappears upstairs and moments later I hear water running. Alrighty. I mean, generally, you don't invite someone over and then leave them to shower. Then I remember Brandon was the one who held up our flight. He's got time management issues. Another reason for me not to like him, as if I needed any more.

Now what do I do? This is so weird. This house is so not Brandon. I wander around the ground floor of the house and find myself in the gym. It's the only room not ensconced in oak. Even the bathroom is oak central. Oak floors, oak beams, and two rows of louvered oak shutters on the floor-to-ceiling windows. An oak vanity. A large oak piece of furniture that looks like a throne mated with a coat rack.

I definitely have to ask him about that.

The home gym is a welcome reprieve. It's the one room that doesn't make me feel like I was dropped in an alternate universe—or decade. Not knowing what else to do with myself, I hop on the treadmill. It's positioned perfectly so you can watch the lake.

Hell, if this were my view, I wouldn't mind running.

I pull my earbuds out of my pocket and slip them in, cuing up my favorite running playlist. Quickly my pace is set and I'm in the zone.

Maybe a little too in the zone.

Maybe so in the zone that I forget that there's another person in this house. A person who sneaks up behind me with the stealth of a ninja—or my music is just that loud over my pounding feet and heart—and scares the crap out of me.

Turning my head to look at him, my rhythm breaks and my foot hovers in the air a fraction of a second too long before making contact with the ground. When it does, it doesn't grab purchase on the belt and immediately sweeps under me. In a split second, my feet whizz off the treadmill, and I'm totally horizontal in the air.

But only for a moment, because I haven't yet mastered the skill of levitation. Before I can blink, I'm smacking down onto the treadmill, my arms useless in breaking my fall. My head bounces once … then twice.

Son of a bitch.

I see stars.

It's not like I've never wiped out running before. No runner can say that. But in front of Brandon Nix …

If my entire body wasn't screaming in pain, I'd probably be mortified. Now it's all I can do not to burst into tears. Instead, I let my body slide off the treadmill into a heap on the floor.

I focus all my energy on that. Andi Nichols doesn't cry, not even when she's given herself a head injury in front of her arch nemesis.

CHAPTER 20: BRANDON

I'd be lying if I said my first reaction wasn't to laugh. I mean, it doesn't matter who it is, wiping out on a treadmill is fuckin' funny. ClikClak is full of viral videos that confirm my viewpoint.

This time it's not funny though. She hit pretty hard, and her head bounced off the treadmill. I spring forward, pulling the stop key as Andi slides off to the floor. She's still for a moment too long, and terror fills me.

I rush to her, scooping her into my arms to get her to a safe location.

"What the hell are you doing? Put me down."

"I'm bringing you out to the couch so I can assess you."

"Are you secretly a doctor? An EMT? In any other way, shape, or form qualified to do anything to my body in a medical sense?"

Obviously, Andi didn't hurt her mouth.

Gingerly I set her down, and she simultaneously shakes her head and rubs her knee.

"No, but I've been evaluated for concussions enough times to know what to do. Maybe I should take you to the hospital."

"I'm not going to the hospital. I'm fine."

She doesn't look fine. She looks shook up. I tell her as much. I try to look at her pupils. I'm not sure what I'm looking for. They look large in the middle of her ice-blue eyes, but otherwise normal.

She rests her head against the back of the couch, cupping her face in her hands. She has angry red scratches on her elbow and on both her knees. "I could use some ice."

I jump up and head to the kitchen. My freezer is stocked with ice packs of all shapes and sizes. "For what part?"

There's silence for a moment. "Um, my whole body?"

I close the door without grabbing one. "Hang on, be right back. Don't fall asleep."

I dash out the side door to where my chiller is nestled under the side eave of the house. I'd planned on using it after Andi left, so I'd already put several frozen 2-liter water bottles in it to lower the temperature. I take the cover off and check the temp. Fifty-five degrees. Not bad for July.

I head back into the house. Andi's still on the couch. Her color looks okay. She's still awake. Her scraped arms and legs aren't bleeding. She doesn't look like anything's broken.

"Give me your phone." I stick my hand out.

"No. Why?"

"Trust me."

"The last thing I do is trust you." She hands me the phone as she says this. I kneel down in front of her and take off her sneakers. Then I scoop her up once more and carry her out the side door.

She must be hurt because she doesn't scream or yell or pound me into oblivion, like I expect her to do. I look at her face to see her watching me with curiosity.

"Aren't you going to ask me what I'm doing with you?"

Andi shakes her head ever so slightly. "I'd fight you if I had the strength. I feel like shit. That really hurt. And it's going to be worse in the morning. Are you just going to deposit my body in my car and roll it into the lake? It might solve a lot of problems for me. Actually, that might be the best solution at this point."

I smile. "I hadn't thought of it, but I'll keep that idea on retainer. It's usually what I do with all the referees who kick me out of games."

She sighs. "It feels like USSLRA is always hiring. Now I know why."

I can't believe she can make a joke at a time like this. I have a feeling she's not going to be laughing when I put her in a vat of ice water. Her eyes grow wide as she spies the ice bath. Her grip tightens on me.

It looks like a cross between a miniature jacuzzi and an oversized cooler that you'd see full of beers in a convenience store. "It's a little bit of an eyesore, but it gets the job done." I look into her blue eyes. They're bright, staring back at me. It feels as if she's staring into my soul. Why have I never seen her look at me like this before? Maybe because there's usually fire pouring out of them. "You ready?"

She nods slightly, and I take that as my cue to lower her in. I feel her tense as her body hits the frigid water. She's submerged to about mid-chest when I hear her swear.

I start to pull her back up a little. "What's wrong?"

She lifts up her arms, scooping her hair up so it doesn't get wet. "I washed it today and actually dried it. It's a good hair day. I don't want it to get wet."

That's what she's worried about?

Without much thought, I extract my hands from around her, pull my favorite red patterned hair tie out of my pocket, and hand it to her. It's one of my favorites, but I don't care. Andi takes it, securing her hair in a loose bun on the top of her head. She still has her earbuds in. I reach forward, gently plucking them from her ears so they don't fall in. As I do, my right hand grazes the side of her jaw.

I freeze, her skin soft under my touch. I don't know why I didn't expect her to be soft. Maybe because she's tough as nails and as physically fit as any professional athlete.

Shaken, I take a step back. "You'll only need a few minutes. Let me go get some towels. I'll be right back." I start to walk away. "Don't drown while I'm gone."

Just inside the door, I stop and let out my breath. I need to put some distance between us if only to calm the boner that's suddenly made an appearance. What the hell? This is Andi Nichols. *Andrew*. She's the ball-busting referee who may have started the end of my career.

As I grab some towels, I try to remember everything I hate about this woman. It's not *her* who's turning me on. It's just that under all that muscle, she's still a woman.

I'm having a natural reaction to an attractive member of the opposite sex. I've been in a dry spell, and my dick is reminding me of that. I grab the fluffy white robe hanging on the back of my door and make my way down to her.

"Your lips are blue." Her teeth are chattering. "How do you feel?"

"Cold." Andi grips the side of the tub and hauls herself to a standing position. I try not to notice how her green shirt clings to her body, revealing a sports bra underneath that does nothing to camouflage her hard nipples. Or how the water sluices down her muscular thighs.

Fuck.

A thousand comments run through my head, starting with "I can see that." Instead, I look away, holding a towel out to her. She grabs it and then reaches for the robe that's draped over my forearm.

When she's finally decent, I turn my gaze back to her. I'm glad she's covered up, but somehow, draped in my robe, her hair haphazardly piled on her head, secured with my hair tie, might be worse.

This is how I imagine she'd look after a night spent tangled in my sheets.

"My head hurts," she says as she secures the sash around her waist. "Got any ibuprofen?"

"Follow me." I nod toward the house, happy to have something else to focus on. We go back into my kitchen. Her teeth are still chattering. She's never going to warm up in those clothes.

"Hang on, let me get you something to change into. We can throw your clothes in the dryer."

I mutter, cursing myself all the way up to my room. This is going from bad to worse. She needs to leave. As soon as she does, I'll whack off and never think of Andi Nichols in a sexual way again. This is simply a biological reaction and nothing else. Any living, breathing man would have the same response.

I am so not attracted to this woman.

I get her the bottle of Advil, grab a T-shirt and some shorts I don't wear anymore because they're too tight in the thighs. I bring them downstairs and put them on the bathroom counter for her. She follows me in, not leaving enough space in between our bodies. At this point, an entire soccer field wouldn't be enough space.

"You're all set in here. I'll get you some water for the Advil." I shimmy around her and close the door behind me.

I swear this woman is cursed. Everything about her spells disaster for me.

CHAPTER 21: ANDI

If you'd asked me to predict how this visit was going to go, I'd never in a million years have picked anything remotely related to an ice bath. Of course, I hadn't predicted helping myself to his home gym and wiping out on the treadmill in the process. But back to the ice bath …

I'm kind of jealous of him. It makes sense that he has one. After a grueling game, it'd be nice to have a quick soak. I have nowhere in my apartment to put one.

That's a first world problem for another day.

Right now, I'm nursing a probable concussion which is not even the worst of it. When I get home, I'll unpack the disaster tonight was. And we haven't even begun to figure out how to solve the initial problem.

Though, it could have been worse. He didn't laugh at me. I would have bet money that Brandon

Nix was the type to laugh when someone fell. Instead he was … well, he's being great. I certainly did not expect a caregiving side to him.

As I slide a faded Boston Buzzards T-shirt over my head and slip into a pair of Brandon's shorts—sans bra and underwear—I realize that this looks bad. Really bad. Like if someone saw me, I might as well toss my entire career in the landfill bad.

There'd be no way to explain this away.

The truth sounds ridiculous.

Every interaction with Brandon Nix takes my situation and moves it from bad to worse. This is probably as bad as it can get.

I look at the bottle of Advil and wonder if I can take the whole thing. My head hurts so bad, I can't imagine that two will even touch it. The room sways a little bit, so I sit down. Seriously, why does he have a wooden throne in the bathroom?

Knock. Knock.

"You okay in there?" The door opens a crack. "Andi, are you—what are you doing?" Brandon stops as he sees me, my hands braced on my knees, willing the room to stop swaying.

"Why do you have a throne in your bathroom?" In the grand scheme of things, this seems like a small, unimportant detail, but for some reason, I have to know.

"It's called a hall tree."

"It looks like the love child of a royal chair and a coat rack."

"Are you okay?"

I look up at him and squint, trying to pull him into focus. "I have a concussion."

He nods. "That's what I was afraid of."

I stand up and pretend that I don't sway like I'm drunk. "I'll be fine. We just need to get this all figured out so I can go home and try to keep myself awake for the next 24 hours."

Brandon turns and I follow him out to the kitchen. "Actually, according to our trainer and team physician, they changed the protocol. Now rest is encouraged because it's healing. You just have to have someone keep an eye on you."

This man knows every weak point I have and how to poke it immediately. How do I admit there's no one to take care of me? I'm not the one who gets taken care of.

"I'll be fine. Let's get this over with so I can go."

Brandon looks at me for a minute before shaking his head. He turns and walks to the table where his laptop sits. He puts his glasses on as he sits down at the oak table. Seriously, was there a deal on oak?

Also, the glasses ...

"This is an interesting table." I can't help myself. It's like my internal filter went flying out of my brain as it rattled around my skull on the treadmill.

Brandon doesn't look up. "I bought the place furnished. Hence the hall tree. I'm not exactly the hall tree type. When I re-do a room, I get rid of what was in there and then add my own stuff. I haven't got to the kitchen yet. Obviously."

That makes so much more sense.

"How long have you lived here?"

He looks around. "Um, six years?" He says it as a question, like I know the actual answer. I look around too. The only room that looks like Brandon is the home gym.

"Cool." I don't know what else to say. Words are swimming around my bruised brain but not forming any sort of cohesive thought.

"Okay, back to why we're meeting." He's all professional. The glasses give sexy businessman vibes. "I was thinking that maybe the only common ground we have is that we both have siblings that mean a lot to us. My sister is currently in recovery from a pill addiction. That's what she's doing in Wyoming. She's on a ranch, trying to stay clean and sober."

Those words cut through the fog. Well, now I feel like a piece of shit.

Also, this makes so much more sense as to why he flew off the handle last night.

I look down at my hands. "I'm sorry. My comments last night were way out of line."

"You were being honest. It's not like I've never thought them myself. Hell, I've thought things that were so much worse. It's something I'm defensive about. I just don't like hearing them from other people. Double standard, I know, but you know how it is with siblings."

I do know how it is with siblings.

His apology goes a long way, but it's still hard to trust someone like Brandon Nix with my career. I decide to take a page from his book and be brutally honest. "I don't really like you, and I'm fairly confident the feeling is mutual. We don't have to like each other, but if we both want to keep our jobs, we need to help each other. If I can't come up with a reason we've been seen together, I'm done forever. The positive spin of a charitable venture may put you back in good graces and take you where you want to go. Do you think you can put on a show and work with me on some benevolent undertaking that will help us both out?"

It feels amazing to say what I'm actually thinking and feeling, instead of keeping it all bottled up.

Brandon keeps looking in his lap. I'm half tempted to stand up and look to see what's so interesting, but I also don't want to invite any lewd comments from him. Also, standing up seems like a lot of work at this moment.

"What do you say?" I gently nudge.

"We need to get this out there fast, don't we?"

I am thinking about my meeting in three short days. "Yeah, but it's probably too little too late for me. I'd like to try even so. I have nothing to lose at this point."

"It'd be nice to create our own organization, but that seems like a lot of work. Maybe we can find an already existing charity and see if we can get involved?" Brandon muses.

He makes a good point. "Can you reach out to your agent or manager and ask them if they can research for you? And then maybe reach out on your behalf? I don't have an agent, but if you can get your foot in the door, you can throw my name in it too. I'm willing to do whatever."

Brandon's laugh is low and bitter. "My agent is the most unlikeable fuckwad you've ever met. He hates me, and there's no way in hell he'd want me to do something that doesn't net the both of us a fat wad of cash."

I want to school my reaction, but that takes more energy than I possess. "Tell me how you really feel."

Brandon takes a deep inhale, indicating a tirade is on the way. While part of me would like to know, a larger part of me wants to die right now, so we need to stay on task.

I interject quickly. "Just kidding. Let's just pick something on our own then."

"What's wrong with your brother?" Brandon asks abruptly.

Concussion or not, his words are like nails on a chalkboard. "Nothing's wrong with him."

Brandon rolls his eyes. "You said he had a terminal illness. What was it again? Something with muscles? I was only half listening. And what's his name?"

Brandon is like so many people who don't realize how it sounds when he asks what's wrong. Benj as a person is perfect. Benj's muscles are another story.

"Benjamin. I call him Benj. He has a disease called Spinal Muscular Atrophy. The nerve cells in his spinal cord that control his voluntary muscles don't work, and it causes his muscles to waste away. It's a genetic thing. When he was born, the life expectancy for his type was maybe upper twenties to early thirties. He's thirty-two and doing so well apparently that he can go on a cross-country road trip with his girlfriend."

"Can he walk?"

"No, he never could. He used to be able to sit on his own, but he's gotten weaker as he's aged. He uses a power wheelchair and will 100 percent run you over if you get in his way. His spine is super curved, and that can have a negative impact on his lungs and breathing. He can feel everything normally, and his cognition is super high. He's way smarter than I am."

"Okay, well your sob story is much better than mine."

I'd take offense, but this is Brandon Nix. I don't think he even knows what it means to think before you speak. On the other hand, he's been surprisingly kind tonight, so maybe I'll cut him some slack this one time.

"I think I should be the judge of that. What's your sob story?"

He pushes his glasses up on top of his head, pulling his hair off his face. "I don't have a sob story."

I smile at his glib attempt at denial. "Your sister's a recovering addict and you said your mom was dead. Of course, there's a sob story."

"You mean like the time my mom and sister were visiting me for my last U18 tournament and my sister was a new driver, but she was pretty good. They were just out driving around between games. It was the middle of the day. They were T-boned by a drunk driver and my mom was killed. Jess was hurt but also saw our mom die a gruesome death, and it messed her up. She became addicted to the pain pills they prescribed her because of her injuries."

My lips form a small O. "I'm sorry."

"Listen, I don't want your pity." He stands up and begins pacing.

"I'm not giving you pity. I'm just saying I'm sorry because it's a sucky thing to have happened. Just like having a brother with a genetic mutation that robs him of movement while keeping his brain totally functioning. It sucks. Sometimes there's nothing more to say than that."

Brandon turns back and looks at me. "I can't believe I'm going to say this, but I agree with you. It fucking sucks."

That it does.

CHAPTER 22: BRANDON

What the hell is going on here? I'm agreeing with Andi Nichols on something? Specifically about my family?

Her situation is different, for sure, but there's a level of tragedy that most people wouldn't understand. Of course, it's not her fault that her brother has a disease. As my dad so likes to remind me, if it weren't for my tournament, my mom and Jess wouldn't have been in Hershey, Pennsylvania, that day to begin with.

I always wanted to counter with, "if you'd have let me play football like I wanted …" but I also know it's pointless to argue with that man. Which is why I need to keep him as far away from this plan as possible.

I look at Andi, who's fading fast. She definitely has a concussion. "Listen, you need to get some rest."

She nods, almost listless. Slowly, she puts her head in her hands.

"Where do you live?"

"Everett."

Fuck, that's north of Boston. "Jesus, what are you doing all the way up there?"

She shrugs. "I have to have quick access to Logan to fly places. It's not like I'm driving down here daily."

"You need to go to the doctor."

"I'll be fine."

"Andrew, you're not fine. I'm taking you to the ER."

She looks up. "You can't. I'll drive myself."

I'm not the brightest bulb, but even I know she should not be getting behind the wheel of a car. She'd be just as bad as a drunk driver. I won't have that on my tally too.

On the other hand, I understand what she's saying. "Hang on, I've got a plan."

"Yikes."

Even with a brain injury, she's still giving me shit. I cannot with this woman. I smile as I grab my phone and call Landon.

"Hey, I need a favor."

There's silence on the line.

"Hello?" I ask. "Landon, are you there? Landon? It's me, Brandon."

"Yes, I'm here," he finally responds. "It's just normally when you call someone, you start with basic pleasantries and greetings, and you don't just launch in with what you want."

"Hello, Landon. How are you this evening? I don't care. I need your help."

"The only reason I'm not hanging up on you right now is that you never ask for help."

When a team works, you become like family. We might fight, but at the end of the day, we're there for each other. I mean, that's how family is supposed to be. My father may not do that, but at least the guys on the Buzzards do. "What's Carlos doing right now? I actually need him."

Landon's boyfriend used to be Callaghan Entay's girlfriend's roommate. Okay, so maybe we're a little incestuous family. All that matters is I can trust Landon and Carlos to be discreet, just like I know I can trust Callaghan and Hannah. There are not many people in that circle.

"Look, I've got a situation. Someone needs a ride to the ER, and I can't bring them."

"What did you do? This is fucked up, man. We're not going to be accomplices to crimes."

I sigh. I hadn't considered how bad this would sound. "I swear, it's not some cloak-and-dagger bullshit. Can you guys come? You'll understand when you get here."

"Is it illegal?"

"Would it matter if it was?"

I can practically picture the gerbils on their wheels inside Landon Stubbs's brain as he mulls this over. "Probably not, but I don't want to end up on some Netflix documentary."

"I swear, it's nothing interesting like that. I'm no Aaron Hernandez. There's no crime. We just need a little discretion."

I disconnect and sit back down at the table with Andi. "Help is on the way. But you also gotta love that people automatically assume I committed a crime." I try to laugh it off.

It's not funny.

"Landon's on his way."

"Landon Stubbs? He can't take me to the hospital either! I don't need to be accused of having inappropriate relationships with two Buzzards players."

"Trust me, you're not Stubbs's type."

She levels her gaze at me. "Gee, thanks."

"Well, considering his boyfriend Carlos is going to be the one to take you to the ER, it's not something I'd take personally."

"Oh. I guess there's nothing I can do about that."

"Trust me, Landon knows how to be discreet. He shouldn't have to be, but that's his bag of rocks to carry, not mine."

She processes this statement for a minute. Her eyes look a little glazed. "Does everyone on the team know?"

I nod. "It's not because of the team. It's a family thing for him. Whatever. Family sucks."

"Family can be great."

"The guys on the team are my family, and even they don't like me that much." As I say it, I realize it's the truth. Normally I pretend that it doesn't bother me. Right now, it does.

I don't have time to get into the touchy-feely crap because Landon and Carlos are at the door. When

Landon walks in and sees Andi Nichols sitting at my kitchen table, he stops cold.

"I had a feeling it was about a woman, but this was the very last thing I imagined." Landon shakes his head.

"So, long story short, Andrew here had a little accident on the treadmill, and we think she has a concussion. She can't drive herself to the ER, but it would look super bad if one of us drove her. Can Carlos take her?"

Carlos smiles at Andi. "Come on, sweetheart. Let's get you into the car." She stands up and gingerly heads toward the door. Her feet are bare.

"Hang on, you need your sneakers." I dash to the living room and grab them. Squatting down in front of her, I open up her shoe so she can easily slide her foot in. She steadies herself with her hand on my shoulder. I tie it and we repeat for the other leg. "Okay, you're good to go."

They walk out to the car. "Carlos, thanks," I call. Carlos looks back at me and nods quickly. He's got his arm around her back, guiding her as she walks slowly. Something about the image rattles around my brain, but I can't figure it out.

It's only when I return to my kitchen that it hits me. Andi's wearing my clothes. It wouldn't be a big deal if it weren't for my last name displayed prominently across her back.

Shit.

CHAPTER 23: BRANDON

I try to avoid Landon's gaze for as long as possible. It lasts approximately 90 seconds.

"What?"

"You owe me an explanation."

"No, I don't."

"No, you don't, but you know I want one."

I laugh. He's one nosy bitch. "So there's been shit going around online that Andi and I are hooking up or whatever. We're not. The plane thing was a total coincidence. But Andi's getting shit apparently and might get fired. Isn't that a load of crap? Can you imagine if we could get fired for who we sleep with?"

Landon levels a look at me.

"Fair point," I concede, "but you know Bob Miller would never fire you for being gay. Coach Janssen wouldn't bench you either. We'd make sure of it."

Landon looks down and nods.

I continue, "So we were trying to come up with a reason why we'd be together that wasn't salacious or cheating."

"And you chose violence?"

"No. I was in the shower, and she decided to use my treadmill. When I came downstairs, I startled her. She wiped out and her head bounced off the treadmill. If she hadn't gotten hurt, it actually would have been pretty funny."

"Why was she in your shirt?"

Shit. If Landon noticed it, then chances are someone at the hospital might too.

"I hope no one else picks up on that."

Landon picks up his phone and types quickly. "I texted Carlos and told him to throw a sweatshirt on her. It'll be fine."

I sag back into my chair. "She was sore, so she hopped in the ice bath. She didn't have anything else to wear. Her clothes are in my dryer." I squeeze my eyes shut as if trying to erase the images of her hard nipples, her scooping her hair up, her in my robe. "It's really innocent, but no one will believe that."

Landon laughs. "I barely believe it, and I know you."

"What's that supposed to mean?"

"Anyone who knows you knows you're honest to a fault. People think you're rude, but you're simply up-front with them. I mean, it comes out rude, but you're not a liar. So if you tell me that nothing's going on between you two, I believe you."

I give my teammate a tight smile.

He continues, "Plus, she's not the type to throw away her career by boning you. Andi Nichols definitely plays by the rules."

"Maybe a little too much by the rules," I mutter.

Landon laughs. "Bitter much? You deserved that card. Frankly, that kick was a red card offense in and of itself, and we both know it."

I mean, Landon's not *wrong* per se, but it's not like I'm going to come out and admit that he's right either.

"Whatever. Andi had an idea that if we work on a charitable cause or something, we can explain our time together that way."

Landon nods. "Sounds good. What charity?"

I scrub my hand down my face. "We never quite got around to figuring that out. We spend most of our time arguing and pissing each other off. We could barely even find any common ground."

"And what's that?"

I sigh. I don't like to talk about my family with guys on the team. Every so often, someone will use it against me, like Trevyon Wallis-Smalls did. We might be teammates now, but the league is transient, and we may not always be.

Opening up just puts ammunition in someone else's gun.

"We both have complicated family lives."

"Who doesn't?" Landon laughs. "I can't even come out to mine."

"That's fucked up, man. You need to tell them. You're happy with Carlos, and they want you to be happy. That's all that matters. But it's different for Andi and me."

Andi and me. Us.

Nope, I will not think of it like that. We're here for one purpose and one purpose only.

"We both have siblings with serious shit."

"That's not a lot to go on."

"Yeah, but it's what we have. Her stuff is a lot worse. Her brother has a disease." As soon the words are out of my mouth, I wish I could pull them back in. Weird, I never feel like that. Not that it's a secret or anything, just that it wasn't my information to share.

It does, however, give me an idea.

I type some keywords into the search bar on my computer, which is still sitting on my kitchen table. A few research papers come up, but not much else. Then I see it. I click on the link and read through it. It's pretty much perfect.

It's as if they were inside my brain and then put it all on a well-manicured website. I know I should wait for Andi to get back, but I've never been any good at waiting. I jot off a quick email to the contact listed before closing my laptop triumphantly.

"You done already? You worked for like five minutes."

I blow on my fingernails and rub them on my shirt. "When you're this good, you don't need to waste a lot of time."

"I feel bad for the women you're with. Some things are better nice and slow."

"I've never had any complaints before." I sit back, crossing my arms over my chest triumphantly.

"You've probably never stuck around long enough to listen to the complaints."

Before we can get into a deep discussion about my ability to satisfy a woman—which I totally can, by the way—the front door opens.

There's no way they can be back already. It's not them. It's just Carlos. "She made me drop her off. I did it only because she promised me she'd call for a ride home. Where is her home by the way?"

I think back. "She lives in Everett."

Carlos swears under his breath. "That's wicked far."

I head through the living room and out to the deck to watch boaters on the lake. Landon and Carlos follow me out. We sit in amicable silence for a while before Carlos's cell phone dings.

"That's my sign. I'm going to pick Andi up. Landon, how are we going to work getting her home?"

I stand up. "I'll go get her. I'll take her to her place. Maybe one of you can pick me up tomorrow morning?"

"You're going to spend the night?" Landon asks.

"Concussion protocol. You can sleep as long as someone watches you. She'll be more comfortable in her own bed." I grab her clothes and keys, heading for the door. "Lock up when you leave, and I'll text you in the morning for a ride." I'm out the door before Landon can object.

Or before I can stop and think through this stupid plan.

CHAPTER 24: ANDI

I hate to say it, but Brandon was right. They do encourage rest after a concussion. They also encourage you to be supervised for the first 24 hours or so. I'm going to listen to the first part of the advice and ignore the second.

Mostly because I don't have anyone to help me out.

It's fine. I'll figure it out.

I text Carlos that I'm being discharged and slowly walk outside to wait. As emergency-room visits go, this was pretty good. In and out in just under two hours. Pretty straightforward.

I've got a handful of paperwork that has me on activity restrictions for at least a week, which means no trip to Birmingham for me. If I'm not in Birmingham, I won't be able to go to Atlanta either.

I mean, I can, technically. Flying isn't out of the question. I'll message Nathan and see what he says.

I have to call out for the game anyway. I'm not supposed to have a lot of screen time, so I'll have to take off from my day job as well.

A mini vacay. All it took was a minor brain injury. Go me.

I see my car pull up. Then I see who's driving it.

Did Brandon not understand what the point of all of this was?

I move as fast as my body permits and slide into the passenger side, keeping my head down while also trying to scan for people recording us. It's dark out now, so it's hard to see much of anything. All this is way too much for my bruised brain to handle. I pull the hood up on the sweatshirt and push my hair over my face instead. I grab the sunglasses off my center console and put them on.

"Why are you here?"

"You need someone to drive you home. I wasn't going to ask Carlos to do that. Plus, he and Landon had plans. We inconvenienced them enough." He's looking straight ahead. "I've got your stuff in the back. What's your address?"

I turn and see my clothes folded neatly.

Brandon Nix touched my underwear.

I should be embarrassed. Instead, I feel a little thrilled.

Oh God, what is happening in my head right now? Are hallucinations and irrational thoughts part of this?

I tell him my address, which he promptly types into his phone. It looks like it belongs in my holder.

He glances over at me. "Just close your eyes and rest. How are you feeling?"

"Like shit. My head hurts. I was nauseous too, but they gave me some Zofran for it."

"Well, while you were off getting all drugged up, I solved our problem."

I recline the seat a little and shift around, trying to get comfortable. "What do you mean, you solved our problem?"

"I found the perfect organization for us to work with."

I lower my sunglasses to look at him. "Explain."

"I figured it had to be a plausible reason that you and I would work together. But it seems like the only thing we have in common is messed up siblings."

I start to protest, but Brandon holds up his hand to silence me. He continues, "You know what I mean. So I found this organization, Ryan's Case for Smiles. They have a whole program that supports siblings of kids with chronic illnesses like cancer."

"My brother doesn't have cancer."

"Yeah, yeah, yeah. They have online stuff and even events for the siblings. Not the kids who are sick, but their brothers and sisters who often get overlooked. You know, the ones who don't get the attention because they're healthy."

"I want to disagree with you, but I don't feel up to it."

"Can't you admit that I hit a home run with this?"

I squint at him, trying to see him more clearly in the darkness. Thanks to the sunglasses, I can barely make anything out. "You made a baseball reference. Shouldn't it be a soccer one?"

"I played baseball too. I wanted to play football, but my mom wouldn't let me."

"I'm trying to picture you playing football. You'd be too small."

"I could have been a running back, back in the day. Those guys are about my size. Or I could have been a kicker or punter."

"You do have quite the boot." I don't mean to compliment him, but it's the truth. I've seen him score a goal on a direct free kick from at least 45 yards. That's totally field goal range.

"What about you? Is there anything you wanted to do that your parents wouldn't let you?"

I try to think. "Nothing's coming to mind. I worked hard in school and tried not to bother them too much. Life was hard enough as it was. I didn't need to add any stress to their lives. I played soccer of course. I couldn't do travel or anything. Just regular school sports. My parents were always there, except on days when Benj had therapy or the weather was bad."

"Isn't a hallmark of playing soccer braving the weather? The school season goes from the heat of summer to snow. Where did you grow up?"

"Benj doesn't do well in weather extremes. Or if it's raining. We lived in South Dakota when I was young, but my parents moved to Denver after Benj was diagnosed, so they could be closer to the specialists. There isn't much in South Dakota, aside from cows."

"I'd think you were exaggerating but I just came from a ranch in Wyoming, so I believe you. There are more cows in Wyoming than people. How old were you when you moved?"

"Almost 11."

"That's a tough time for an upheaval. I started traveling at about 12. I went to live with a host family because we didn't have a competitive enough league where we lived, and my father wasn't going to uproot just for me. I ended up in the USSL Training Academy and playing for the USSL U18 team. I was initially drafted by the Sacramento Saints before being traded to the Nevada Renegades and then the Boston Buzzards."

"You were on the National team as a youth?"

"Yeah, before I hit the adult league. I was … a bit of a shit show from 18 until about 20. If Sacramento hadn't already had me under contract, I don't think I would have had a career. I still played, of course, but things were a little dicey then. Lots of people gave me a pass because of the accident and all."

"So, you're saying you're settled down then?" I find that hard to believe.

"Off the field, yes. On the field, I play with the same amount of passion I always have."

"Why are you like that during games?" If asked about this later, I'll claim I don't remember. He's being so open that it might be my only shot to find out.

"Like what?"

"Such an asshole." Okay, I'm definitely blaming that on the head injury.

"My dad once said I need to leave it all on the field or not bother walking to the locker room."

"Okay, I can see that, but you're ... a little over the top."

"What do you mean by that?"

How do I phrase this without sounding like a total jerk? "You say whatever's on your mind, all the time. Even if it's offensive or hurts someone's feelings."

His hand is up again. "I can't live my life worrying about how everyone else is feeling. That's their issue, not mine. I tell it like I see it."

I shake my head before remembering that I shouldn't. "Your agent must have a field day with you."

"My agent is a dick, and he hates me."

There's that blunt truth. "Don't sugar coat it for me."

"I'm not saying anything that's not 100 percent the truth. My agent is the world's biggest dick."

"Are you trying to be a close second?"

He shrugs, his thumbs tapping on the wheel to some imaginary song. "You know what they say, 'like father, like son.'"

If I were driving, I'd probably swerve the car off the road right now. Good thing I'm in the passenger's seat. "Your dad is your agent?" Maybe my ears aren't working properly. They said I could develop tinnitus. While that's normally a ringing in the ears, maybe it changes the way words sound.

"Yeah, he doesn't like me much. I mean, if your own father doesn't care for you, then you don't have high expectations for the rest of the world."

"I'm sorry, I cannot relate at all to that. How can a father not love his own son?" I think about my dad carrying Benj around, changing him, feeding him. How he built special equipment just so Benj could do as much as any other kid. "I'm sorry," I say again.

"Don't be sorry. It's made me who I am. Nothing bothers me. It's better that way. I don't get all bent out of shape about stupid things."

I want to object. There's something at the edge of my brain that is scratching to get out. Before I can think of it, the directions have Brandon turning down my street.

As he shifts into park in my driveway, I unbuckle my seatbelt and open the car door. "Well, thanks for the ... wait, how are you getting home?"

"Someone'll pick me up tomorrow before workout."

I whip off my sunglasses only to put them back on. Damn, that streetlight is bright. "Excuse me? You're not staying here."

He reaches in the back and grabs my clothes. *Brandon Nix is touching my underwear again.*

"I am, because I know damn well those discharge instructions say to be supervised."

He's not wrong.

"Unless you can tell me who's going to check on you all night, let's go inside, lest we're spotted. Again."

The only thing that's worse than hating this man because he's so wrong is hating him because he's right.

CHAPTER 25: BRANDON

I don't know what I expected Andi Nichols's place to look like, but this isn't it. She lives on the ground floor of a multi-family house that's nothing to look at. Some might even call it an eyesore. It's not that it's unkempt or run down. It's probably been renovated in recent history. It's just … something's missing.

"This place doesn't have enough windows on the front side. It looks off balance or something." I stare up, trying to figure out why it looks so unattractive.

"Maybe you have too many windows."

That's a weak argument, but she does have a brain injury, so I'll let it slide this time. "I have the right number of windows. Which door is yours?"

"I'm on the left. I don't care about the outside. I don't spend any time out there. What's important is that this condo is super expensive, and I have virtually no room."

I think she made a joke.

"At least you have off-street parking," I offer.

She smiles. "That was a big seller, though I sort of wish for a garage during the winter." She puts the key in the lock and pushes the door open. "And I'm not going to lie, now I totally want an ice bath."

The place is sparkling clean and has obviously been refinished this century. It doesn't even look like someone lives here. It's narrow, half the width of the house. You can see straight to the back where the kitchen is. The floors are shiny oak, and the rest of the place is white. White walls. White cabinets. What's not white is gray. Gray appliances. Gray furniture. The bare minimum of everything. There are no rugs. No toss pillows. One lone blanket covers the back of the couch. It looks like the same decor you'd find in a hotel room. It is totally devoid of personality.

On second thought, this place suits Andi Nichols perfectly.

Or at least that's what I would have thought before today. She has a personality. She just keeps her cards close to her chest. Real close.

"Listen, it's nice that you drove me home and all." She pauses and looks around, still wearing her sunglasses. "But this is only a one bedroom. I mean, technically there's a second bedroom, but it's my office. There's not a bed in there or anything."

"Yeah, mine is too. My second bedroom is a gym, which you know all about. What's your point?"

"I need to sleep. I'm really tired."

"Okay, go to sleep. I'll be out here on the couch."

"I can't make you sleep on the couch."

"You're not making me do anything. I don't know if you know this, but no one makes me do anything I don't want to do. I can sleep pretty much anywhere. I can sleep on the couch. The floor. I could sleep in a kitchen chair. Hell, I can sleep standing up if I need to. My sleep is very important to me, and I don't let my environment control it."

She stands there.

"Andrew, I'm serious. You saw me on the plane. I can sleep anywhere. Now you go get some rest. Your body's been through a lot today." I put my hands on her shoulders and gently steer her toward the door that has to be the bedroom.

Once she's over the threshold, I go out to the kitchen to get her some water and maybe a snack. Her kitchen is predictably neat and tidy. The fridge is well stocked with lots of fruits and vegetables, all in meal-prep containers.

She seems like the type to meal-prep.

There are also several prepared meals in there from a service.

Indeed, Andi Nichols has her shit together.

I grab her a bottle of water as well as some crackers. Are crackers the right choice? She doesn't have a stomach bug, and she's not hungover either. Maybe she shouldn't be eating? I google "what to eat when you have a concussion."

Apparently, it's a diet high in good fats, not dissimilar to the Mediterranean diet, FYI. I put the crackers back and make her some whole grain avocado toast with a side of almonds. I was right about the water. Hydration is important.

When I bring the plate and cup to her room, it's dark. It takes my eyes a minute to adjust to the lack of light. I see Andi curled up on her side. She's still wearing the sunglasses. From the sounds of her breathing, I'd guess she's sleeping. I quietly walk over and put the toast and water down on her nightstand. Gingerly I pull the glasses off her face and put them there as well. I pull the light gray blanket that's neatly folded across the end of the bed up over her body. I back out of the room and pull the door mostly shut.

Then, because I wasn't lying about my sleep being important and being able to sleep anywhere, I set my alarm for two hours later. I'll check on her every two hours until morning.

Maybe it should be one hour.

Andi Nichols can't die on my watch. That would be bad. Very bad.

I adjust my alarm and lie down on her couch. There's a large square ottoman that I pull up to create a wider area for more comfort. I pull the gray blanket down off the back of the gray couch and wonder what this woman has against color.

Never in a million years would I have predicted where this night would land. Mostly I never would have predicted the way Andi would have landed on my treadmill, but that's not the point.

Okay, it was actually pretty funny, and I'm kicking myself for not getting that on video. Not that we need anything else going viral out there. It's why we're in this mess in the first place.

There's a light at the end of the tunnel. I can't wait for her to be a little more coherent so I can share with her the news about the charity I found. I emailed them to see what we can put together. Maybe a soccer clinic or a game or something? I'll probably have to check with the front office to see what the policy is, but I know lots of players use official Buzzards swag for charities.

For a minute I feel like a shit that I've been playing all this time and haven't done anything for charity. In my defense, it's usually the agents or managers who set that up. My dad doesn't want anything going to anyone unless it's him.

I close my eyes, drifting off like my body's used to doing. I start awake to the chiming of my alarm, groggy and not believing an hour has already passed. I open Andi's door a crack. She's in the same position. I cross the room in two steps putting my hand over her collarbone hoping to feel some movement. I let out a sigh of relief when it slowly rises and then falls under my palm.

I keep it there for a few more moments, making sure her breathing is rhythmical and steady. Content that she's doing okay for the moment, I return to the living room, ready to repeat this procedure every sixty minutes throughout the night.

Despite my previous claims, I can't fall back asleep. I putter around on my phone, making lists about ideas I have for our public image reboot. There are always the typical fancy-pants fundraisers that we could certainly help with. Appearances and signing memorabilia or something.

I bet I could get Callaghan Entay to help me out with a fundraiser. He did something like that where he signed autographs for charity. Xavier Henry's wife, Ophelia, made Landon and me take Hannah to the function for Callaghan. She was not exactly a willing participant.

In the end, they got together and now they're all lovey-dovey and bullshit. So's Henry with his wife, which started as a fake marriage. It's funny, Henry and Ophelia had to convince the world they were in love. Andi and I have to convince the world we're not.

This is a messed-up time we live in, all thanks to social media like ClikClak. Well, since social media created this mess, we should definitely use it to clean it up.

Except … I don't know anything about posting there. I mainly use it to see what people are saying about me and to watch funny videos of people falling. And the occasional pimple popping.

I know it's gross, but I can't look away.

I look up Andi, but she doesn't have a public account. But the videos talking about the two of us …

Now I know why she's desperate.

There's no way she's keeping her job.

This is complete and utter bullshit. There's nothing going on between us, other than I'm a decent human being who's trying not to let someone die on my watch. Speaking of which, it's time to check on her again.

Andi's leg is twitching. Is it a normal sleep thing or a seizure? I turn on the bedside lamp and sit down on the other side of the bed to watch her for a moment. I'm not comfortable, so eventually I shift so I'm propped up against the headboard. This is much better. Did I mention there are no pillows on the couch? I've never met a female without tons of useless pillows around.

The motion in her legs stops and she rolls over toward me. "You okay, Andrew?" I whisper. I don't know why I called her that. Maybe because in the middle of the night, in the soft glow from her lamp, with her sleeping next to me, this feels more intimate than it should.

She mumbles something that sounds like an affirmative response.

"Okay, I was just checking on you. I'll go back to the couch now." I start to get up.

She mumbles again, this time the word is more clear. "Stay."

I freeze, one leg hanging over the side of the bed. My gut clenches. Does she really want me to stay in her bed with her? It's not like anything's going to happen. I'm here for her. To make sure she's okay. I still need some sleep.

That's all this is. Sleep.

I close my eyes, knowing I'll open them again in a few minutes.

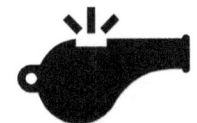

CHAPTER 26: ANDI

My head hurts.

There's avocado toast wilting on my nightstand. How the hell did that get there?

At the hospital, they told me I could have some memory loss. I didn't expect it to be this bad. How could I not remember making avocado toast? It's like a four-step process and includes the use of a sharp knife. Maybe I shouldn't be here alone.

I'm curled up on my side staring at the food on my nightstand with absolutely no recollection of how it got there. All I remember is having weird dreams about a dog—I think it was a corgi from one of Hannah LaRosa's videos. I was chasing after it, trying to give it a red card. No matter how many times I yelled at it to stay, it just kept running away.

My heart stops when I feel the other side of the bed depress with movement, like a dog jumped up on it.

Except I don't have a dog, unless Sir Fluffybottom really is here.

I glance behind me.

What the hell is Brandon Nix doing in my bed?

"What the hell are you doing in my apartment? Why are you in my bed?"

"Isn't this a condo? Would you call it an apartment?"

I blink slowly. Is he really arguing with me about this?

I'm so disarmed that I answer his questions for lack of anything else to say. "I guess technically it's a condo, but I feel stupid saying that. When you say condo, people think of high rises with shiny amenities. This is so not that. They just say condo so they can collect an HOA fee. It doesn't matter. Why are you here? You're in my bed!" I pull a blanket up around me, as if to cover myself in modesty. It doesn't matter that I'm fully dressed.

"Making sure you don't die. That would not help our case." He stretches out, placing his arms behind his head. Like he belongs here. *Like he should be comfortable in my bed!*

"I'd be dead. I wouldn't care."

"Yeah, but they'd probably try to pin your death on me. I don't think my career can withstand that kind of scandal."

"Fair point, but why are you in my bed?"

"You said stay," he says matter of factly.

Never in a million years would I invite Brandon Nix into my bed. "No way. I did no such thing."

"You did. I came in to check on you, but you said stay. I thought maybe you were afraid or not feeling well, so I stayed. Again, I can't have you dying on my watch. I don't watch enough Dateline to know how to dispose of your body without tracing it back to me. Just my hair alone will incriminate me. It sheds all the time."

I have to laugh at this absurd situation as well as his comments about his locks. "Your hair is a crime in and of itself. But don't worry; you're a dude. You get an automatic pass. You'd be fine." I stand up and head to the bathroom. When I finish up and open the door, he's sitting on my couch like he owns the place, scrolling away on his phone.

He keeps talking as if there'd been no break in the conversation. As if he belongs here. As if this is something *we do.* As if it's normal for us to share a bed. "What was that supposed to mean? Do you really think I could accidentally kill you and get away with it just because I'm a male athlete?"

This is an easy argument to win. I don't even have to visit Google to come up with a list of offenders. "Michael Vick. Oneil Cruz. Ray Lewis. O.J. Simpson."

Seriously, what the hell is wrong with our society?

"Michael Vick didn't kill anyone. It was just dog fighting."

"Yeah, and he was permanently suspended, except then he wasn't, and he ended up not only playing again, getting paid millions of dollars, but even winning a courage award from his teammates.

The other three absolutely killed people, and two of them kept playing after the fact! I can't even get paid the same amount as my coworkers simply because I don't have a penis. Now I'm going to lose everything I've ever wanted because some hot soccer player invades my personal space, and the collective internet expects me to swoon like a ninny."

"You think I'm hot?" Brandon asks with a shit-eating grin. He stands up and disappears into my kitchen.

Of course, he focuses on that. "You know what you look like, though someday we have to circle back to what's going on with your hair. Did you even hear what I said? The rest of it? I ..." I plop down on my couch. "I don't know what to do with you." The last statement is more a mutter to myself.

He sits down next to me and hands me a glass of water. "First you can drink this because you have to stay hydrated, and then you can thank me because I've solved our problems. Do you have a computer?"

I point to the second bedroom that serves as my office. "Laptop's on the desk in there. Just grab it and bring it out." I'm pretty sure that even without my permission, Brandon would have helped himself. He has boundary issues, which is a shock to exactly no one. I do drink the water though, not that I'd tell him I'm thirsty.

Actually, I wouldn't tell anyone I was thirsty because I wouldn't want to put them out or draw attention to myself. In this case, though, I don't want Brandon Nix to know he was right.

I'd probably rather turn to dust right in front of him than admit that he was right about something, especially my needs.

He returns with my computer and opens it up. He turns it toward me so I can enter my passcode. As he does he says, "We also need to circle back to the pay comment." Brandon opens up a browser and hits a few keystrokes. "Voila!" he says triumphantly. "This is what we need. I tried telling you about it last night, but you were having trouble focusing. I already emailed them and took care of everything."

I blink at the screen. I'm not supposed to have a lot of screen time. I don't know what I think will happen if I look at it. The scene in *Raiders of the Lost Ark* where the guy's face melts off passes through my mind.

Probably not that.

I hope.

"Pillowcases?" I squint, trying to read the small print.

"The main thing is pillowcases for kids with chronic illnesses like cancer, but they have this whole other section for siblings of kids with chronic illnesses. They do counseling and groups and special gifts because these kids are often overlooked. Did you know there's a term for that? It's called glass child syndrome. It's because the parents of children with special needs tend to 'look through' their healthy children."

I feel my breath rush out, leaving a hollow feeling in my chest.

It's perfect.

Don't cry. Don't cry. Don't cry.

I squeeze my eyes shut, willing the sudden moisture to be reabsorbed into my body. It sounds ridiculous but it's a maneuver I perfected when I was a kid.

No one wants to see the healthy one crying about anything. We have no reason to cry.

"I'm going to stop in the front office to see about doing an event. Like a clinic or something. You know, teach them how to play soccer. And then we can have the kids come to a game. Make a big deal for them."

It takes me a bit longer to process what he's saying. "That's all well and good for repairing your image, but what about me? Why am I here? I mean, other than I live here. What does this have to do with me?"

Brandon's brow furrows behind his glasses. They really are a good look for him. Kind of a Clark Kent vibe. If Clark Kent had a kid with Tarzan and that kid only wore flip-flops.

"I was thinking at the clinic there could be a referee station. Like some kids could play and other kids could ref. You can't have a game without referees, you know. Anyway, I'll talk to my people when I'm done with my workout." Brandon gets up and starts looking around. "I've got to get going. I'm going to be late as it is."

It takes me a minute to realize what he's searching for. "You don't have keys. You drove my car."

"Damn it, that's right." He pulls out his phone and rapidly texts. "Shit. I was supposed to text

Landon to come pick me up this morning, but he won't have time to get up here and back before we're supposed to be there. I don't care about being late—"

"I know," I interject. It is really something I hate.

He rolls his eyes and continues, "But I can't make Landon late. They fine us. I mean, I could always just pay his fine. It's only money."

"Says the person who has plenty of money."

"I don't want to get him in trouble. It's fine if they're mad at me. They can't be mad at him, too." He looks around as if trying to formulate another plan.

I sigh. "Just take my car. We can figure out how to get it when you're done working. I'm calling in anyway. I've got to cancel my trip to Birmingham."

That's something I dread doing. Nathan's going to think I'm faking to get out of the meeting. I don't like facing difficult situations, but running away only creates more problems.

I stand there and take it like a woman.

Once the door closes with Brandon Nix on the other side, I feel like I can breathe a little more. I also feel totally gross, so I take a lukewarm shower as per my instructions. Then I send the email I've been dreading.

Hi Nathan,

I had an accident while running on a treadmill last night. I have a concussion. I'm afraid I won't be able to do the Birmingham game, as I'm on a ten-day restriction of physical activity. I can still fly down to

Atlanta if you need me to. I would only ask that one of the USSLRA administrative assistants book my tickets. I'm supposed to be on total screen rest for the next two days at least. I'll check my email periodically, or feel free to give me a call with your directives.

Andi

P.S. I'm attaching the discharge paperwork from the hospital for my personnel file. Please let me know if you need other documentation.

I like throwing directives in there. It's a union thing. I really should email them too, but I'm sleepy again. I'll lie down here for a bit. After a short nap, I'll email my union rep and let them know about the impending meeting.

And then maybe I'll think about what happened with Brandon Nix.

Just a quick nap.

CHAPTER 27: BRANDON

I never truly understood the expression "you could knock me over with a feather" until I saw it written all over Leora Deventhorpe's face. Leora is the Boston Buzzard's public relations person, and apparently, I was the last person she ever expected to see asking to schedule a charity event.

When I gave her the Post-it with the website and told her my ideas, she stared at me, her mouth hanging open.

"So, I want to do a soccer clinic for both prospective players and referees. They've done a similar event with the Philadelphia Flyers before. Then, can we have the kids and their parents attend the game? You know, give them all sorts of free shit and maybe even have them come down on the field. Make a big deal out of them. It's got to suck having a brother or sister who's sick all the time. The sick one gets the attention. Never the healthy one."

Leora doesn't say anything, so I keep talking. "I mean, maybe the Buzzards could sponsor their gala or something? I saw it on the website. Something about red sneakers. But that's for the sick kid part. I want to focus on the JustSibs part of it, mostly."

Finally, she remembers how her mouth works as she closes it and swallows. "I can check the calendar. Usually these things are scheduled a few months out at minimum. So that would put us in September or October. Probably don't want to go too much later in the year than that."

"That's great," I say, my smile wide. "I emailed their person to get information. Can I send that to you so you can do … what you do here?" I look around her small office, not sure exactly what she does. "Work your magic." I cover, not wanting to seem as ignorant as I am.

I probably should know, but in the five years I've been with the Buzzards, I don't think I've done anything public relations related. Certainly not anything for good.

This one, I blame on my dad. He's managed my career since I was a kid. Not only is he not getting me endorsements, he's not even helping me with my public image. He's letting me flail and fail on my own, probably so he doesn't have to take ownership.

He's good at that.

I don't want to be like that.

I turn back. "Hey, Leora, I'm sorry if I've been a little bit of trouble with my image and all."

The shocked expression is back. I leave it at that and head for Andi Nichols's Ford Escape. It's in good shape—for a Ford—but it's not new. I check the odometer. It's got almost 100,000 miles on it.

She's lucky this is still running.

It reminds me of my old Explorer. My mom's Explorer.

Her place is tiny too. How much do referees make anyway? Plus, she said she still has a day job. This doesn't make sense. I'll have to ask her why she's so stingy with her money.

What did she mean by not getting paid as much as her male counterparts? I had to have misunderstood. Surely that's got to be illegal.

I have so many questions for her.

I meet up with Callaghan outside the training facility. He's going to follow me up to Andi's so I can drop her car off and then give me a lift home. There's a small circle of people who can know about Andi and me.

I say that like we're a couple.

Ha. That will never happen. I'd never want that to happen. Even if she is more interesting than I thought. And more attractive. Much more attractive.

The image of her soaking wet pops into my brain again.

Yeah, no. Not in a million years. Not if she were the last woman on Earth. She's nothing but a hard-ass, ball-busting, prim and proper rules follower. That's not my type.

She meal preps and has fresh avocados for Christ's sake. Who lives like that?

That's not the kind of life I want. Her apartment is sterile and devoid of personality. My place may be entirely made of oak, but at least it doesn't feel like the inside of a hotel.

I mean, my place doesn't feel like me either, but I don't know what I'm supposed to feel like. Something's always been off. The only one who made me feel even kind of grounded was my mom. Then she was gone, and Jess was recovering—and then spiraling out of control.

Jess had always been a daddy's girl, so the chaos she created turned him into a cold shell of a human. To be clear, he wasn't warm and fuzzy to begin with, but he's become a downright ass ever since.

He made it easy not to have a home.

It's one reason why I think I liked my house when I first looked at it. It was old and lived in, but it felt like a home. Maybe not mine, but someone's. I had to start somewhere.

Not belonging anywhere—or to anyone—makes it easy for me to speak my mind. I don't care what people think about me because it's not like they're going to be there in the end.

Or even the next day.

"Don't hurt yourself," Callaghan says from the driver's seat. We just dropped Andi's car off. I used her keys and let myself in to check on her. She was sleeping again, but she stirred when I shook her shoulder.

I could have sworn she mumbled something like, "Don't touch me." It was enough to tell me she was in her right mind. I crept quietly out, leaving the keys on the hook by the door.

Because of course, she has a hook for her keys.

"Andi doesn't like me."

"You call her Andrew."

"Nicknames are a form of affection." I don't know why this is my response. I didn't give her a nickname because I felt any sort of affinity. Quite the opposite, really. I did it to piss her off. It's fun watching her get all riled up.

She doesn't rile easily.

In fact, I'd say most of the time, she doesn't have much of a reaction at all. But when she does … whatever. She's not my concern.

"I think I shocked Leora Deventhorpe with wanting to sponsor a charity event."

"Let's face it, you're not usually the first in line to volunteer or shake hands. Do you even sign autographs?"

"Well, I take selfies and I even smile." That's a dig at Callaghan. His panties were in such a twist after he—we—blew the quarterfinals last year that he told a bunch of cleat chasers that he'd only smile when there was something to smile about.

He went viral for that, and not the good kind of viral way.

See? I'm not the only one. This social media thing really is a double-edged sword.

"I mean, it wouldn't hurt to get good publicity for once."

"You're on that thin ice?" Callaghan glances over at me, raising his eyebrows.

"I thought you'd be in the know, being captain and all. I'm on probation. I don't know exactly what that means, but I'm guessing they're not going to be super tolerant of me fucking up much more."

"I'd guess not. That's the problem in our field. There's always someone else, younger, healthier, more driven, ready to take our spot on the team."

I shrug. I have no idea what I'd do if I didn't play soccer, but the thought of not playing again doesn't gut me the way it does Callaghan.

And the thought of not playing gutted Xavier Henry too. I don't know him that well, since he just joined the team, but we all know—now—that he married a stranger to be able to keep playing in the USSL.

Hell, if I'd ever do something so desperate.

On the other hand, when I try to think about life without soccer, my heart rate picks up speed. Soccer's been the one constant in an otherwise tumultuous life, even though soccer was the cause of the chaos to begin with.

"What would you do if you weren't playing soccer?" I ask.

Callaghan says nothing.

"Oh, come on. Your shoulder has been messed up for months. You've had to be thinking about it."

"It's all I ever think about. I'm not getting any younger. Now that I've had my caps with the National Team, I'm probably going to work on transitioning away. CC needs to get more experience. I'm working with Max a bit more on goalkeeping coaching. I'm not trying to push him out of a job, but it's a logical step. I'll probably go to another team to be their keeper coach, if I can get hired somewhere."

I laugh. "I don't think anyone in their right mind will hire me for a coach. I've got a few years to figure it out."

"How old are you?"

"Thirty-two."

"Really?" His eyebrows elevate. "I thought you were much younger. You act that way."

Fair point.

Callaghan continues, "There's an old saying in football, 'Act like you've been there before.'"

I interject. "That's about scoring. You know, not excessively celebrating. Act like it's no big deal, and it's what you expect. Vince Lombardi said it. And that's how I do act." I know my football trivia, especially that about the legendary Packers coach. Hell, the Superbowl trophy is named after him.

"Okay, well, act like a professional then. On and off the field."

Entay's trying to be helpful; I'm sure he is. Still, it chafes at me, and I don't know why. It shouldn't be that hard, right?

CHAPTER 28: ANDI

It wasn't a quick nap. When I wake up, it's dark out. I look at my watch—9 p.m.

On the one hand, I feel much better. The headache is down to a dull roar, and some of the fog has lifted. I'm hungry.

I toss the avocado toast that was still on my nightstand. Seriously, how did it get there? Then it dawns on me. Brandon must have made it.

My suspicions are confirmed when I see the state of my kitchen. There's a cutting board still on the counter that has the avocado rind and seed still out, along with a knife and fork. There are toast crumbs on my counter.

This is so not how I roll.

In the span of 24 hours, Brandon Nix has completely immersed himself in my life. He's been in my kitchen. In my bed! He even picked the charity we're going to be working with. I'd never have picked this one. I'd have done something with SMA or Muscular Dystrophy or something for Benj. Not something for me.

And he still has my car, to boot! Which means he has to come back here, risking even more chances of being seen together.

This could ruin my life.

But as I look out my window, I see my car's back. The keys are on the hook next to the door where they belong. He thinks he can just come in here whenever he wants? The audacity of that man.

I cross my arms in a huff, only because I'm alone with no one to witness my tantrum or judge me for it.

Also because I'm having a lot of feelings right now and have no idea what to do with them all.

With way too much force behind my movements, I swipe at the mess on the counter. But as I pick up the avocado seed, something inside me cracks, causing tears to spring to my eyes.

Brandon Nix made me avocado toast. He stayed the night and took care of me. Or at least he made sure I didn't die. He slept next to me because he thought I asked him to. And he found a charity for me.

Not my brother. Not kids like him.

Kids like me.

It's like he sees me.

What did he call it? Glass child syndrome? Ironic, because he's the first person not to see right through me.

I put my hand over my chest which feels tight. I hope this is another sequela of the concussion, though I fear it's not.

I fear it's something much, much worse. I sink down on my couch, my head resting on the back of it.

I don't remember the last time anyone saw me. Even if they tried, I don't let myself be seen.

Not that anyone tries real hard. They hit the wall I've so carefully constructed and then turn and walk away. They don't even bother looking for the door. It's what Mike did.

Yet somehow, Brandon has come barreling full force at me like the Kool-Aid man.

It's not like these are feelings or anything. It's the novelty of being seen. Brandon Nix is still Brandon Nix. He's unapologetically rude and crude.

Except he's not exactly crude.

And he's more blunt than rude.

He's a blowhard, that's for sure.

But he's smart. And surprisingly compassionate.

And he's knocking on my door.

Not metaphorically knocking at my emotional door. Actually knocking on my physical door. I may only have one window in the front of the house, but it is right next to the door and my couch sits in front of it. Sure as God made little green apples, Brandon Nix is standing on my doorstep.

What could he possibly want now?

I haul myself up and pull open the door. "What are you doing here?"

"Checking on you and hello, Andrew."

"Would you please stop calling me that?" Normally I would let it roll off me, like I do with so many other things, but this is not a normal situation. I don't know what it is, but it's definitely not normal. "And I'm fine. You don't have to be here. You shouldn't be here. What happens if people see you coming and going?"

"We're working on the event, of course."

I'm confused. This is all hypothetical and in the air. He's talking like it's a done deal.

He leans in and whispers in my ear, "I'm just saying that in case your place is bugged or if the head of the USSLRA is out in the bushes listening. I still have a suspicion that you're a secret spy or something." His breath is hot on my neck, sending shivers down my spine. "Though, in reality, I did talk to Leora in the front office today, so this is going to happen."

I try to remember what *this* he's talking about, but I can't seem to focus on anything but how close he is to me.

He doesn't have bad breath right now. In fact, he has that cool spicy smell associated with men's deodorant and shaving cream. I close my eyes and try to covertly inhale—

What the hell am I doing?

I jump up and stumble back. I must have lost my mind. Maybe it's the concussion. Maybe it's bleeding in there. That's got to be the only logical explanation.

"Andrew, what's wrong? You're really pale."

I look around my place, trying to see if anything else is weird. Everything looks how it's supposed to. Everything smells how it's supposed to. It's just ... him.

I'm now so aware of him.

"Have you ever had a concussion before?" I ask. I don't know what else to do. I've got to get to the bottom of what's going on.

"Sure. Too many to count."

His answer stuns me. That's not good. Not at all. Not with all the research that's come out about chronic traumatic encephalopathy. It's an area of interest for me since it was first researched at Boston University, where I got my physical therapy degree. "Aren't you worried about CTE?"

"Ehh," he says with a shrug. "I mean, I should be, but there's not as much out there about CTE in soccer players. The irony is I never wanted to play soccer. I wanted to play football. At least in football, you get to wear pads and helmets."

Brandon looks at me and closes the gap between us. He takes my hands in his. "You're freaking out. What's going on?"

I close my eyes, unable to look at him. Swallowing hard, I raise my lids and meet his gaze. We're as close as we were when I gave him that red card. "I think I'm having hallucinations." The smell—his scent—is still there, calling to me. I tilt my head forward and inhale again.

It's as if the notes of fresh air and sea, infused with mint and pine, awaken something deep within me. Very deep, mostly located at the center between my legs.

Maybe, if I hold very still, this moment will pass, my rational sense will return, and Brandon Nix will never be the wiser.

"Did you just smell me?"

Where this man is concerned, luck is never on my side.

I don't move a muscle. "I'm gonna say no." Even as I say it, I feel the flush creeping up my neck, warming my cheeks. My hands, still trapped in his, are beginning to sweat.

He leans in and whispers in my ear. "It sure seemed like you smelled me."

I close my eyes again, his cheek millimeters away from mine, his mouth next to my ear. My breath is starting to come in short pants. "I was trying to see if I had a sense of smell."

Brandon laughs, a big throaty chuckle. "You have a concussion, not COVID."

I don't know if I've ever heard him laugh like this before.

I pull back to look at his face. His eyes are crinkled at the corners, years of playing soccer in the sun etching lines. His dark eyes twinkle mischievously. I lick my lips when my gaze gets to his mouth.

"It could be COVID," I stall.

"Do you have a fever?" Now he licks his lips.

"It certainly feels warm in here." Sweat prickles my skin.

Brandon leans in and blows gently on the side of my neck.

Holy hell.

Did I just orgasm?

Wait—what the hell is going on here? This is Brandon Nix. I should not be thinking about him and orgasms in the same paragraph, let alone in the same sentence. Yet somehow, as his hands stroke up my arms, one landing firmly on the back of my neck, that's all I can think about.

CHAPTER 29: BRANDON

This is not why I came here tonight. She did this. She smelled me. Everyone knows that's an automatic green light.

But this would be bad. Kissing her would be the exact wrong thing to do. It doesn't matter how much I want to.

And I do.

I clear my throat and take a step back, my hands dropping away. There needs to be some space between us. Like a few states.

"What's going on here?" Andi finally says in a hoarse voice.

"I just stopped by to check on you."

"I'm still breathing," she all but pants.

"Quite heavily, I may add." I smile.

Andi takes a step back too. "This … is not what I expected." She sits down on the couch, somewhat dazed. I'm almost certain it's not because of her concussion. I sit down as well, leaving a respectable six inches between us.

"Okay, well, now I know you're alive and well. I can probably go." I glance at her out of the corner of my eye.

"That would probably be best."

"Did you let work know you're out for the week?" I don't know why I ask her this. It's none of my business. It's almost as if I'm stalling, like I don't want to leave.

"Yeah. I canceled my trip to Birmingham. I have to see if they still want me in Atlanta."

"Who's playing in Atlanta?"

"No one. I'm supposed to meet with Nathan Forget at USSLRA headquarters."

This doesn't sound good. In all honesty, I thought she'd been blowing this whole thing out of proportion. If they're calling her in for a meeting, then probably not.

"That's not good."

"No, it's not."

"Tell them about the thing we're doing. We have nothing to hide. Nothing's happened that shouldn't have."

"Except you're sitting on my couch right now."

I stand up. "Tell me who else you have arranged to come and check on you, and I'll leave." I cross my arms over my chest. "I'll wait."

It's kind of sad that she doesn't have anyone.

"My parents will text or call me."

"Are they back from their trip yet?"

She shakes her head. "They'll be back in two days."

"Then I'll stop checking on you in two days."

I head for the door, knowing this is the absolute right thing to do, even though it's the last thing I want to do. I pull open the door, and then turn back over my shoulder. "What would you do if I kissed you right now?"

Andi's lips part, a breath whooshing out of them. "I'd hate you even more than I already do."

"Because you know you'd love it." And with that, I close the door and stride to my car.

It's only once my car hits I-93 south that I finally exhale. That was reckless. That was stupid. That was classic Brandon Nix, thinking I can say whatever I want and do whatever I want to get whatever I want.

I'm just like my sister.

It occurs to me that maybe I am. Except instead of being addicted to pain pills, I'm very quickly becoming addicted to a certain blonde referee who doesn't put up with my bullshit.

If you'd offered me a million dollars at any point between the moment Andi gave me my red card and right now, I would not have predicted ending up at this point, unable to keep her out of my thoughts. Wondering what she tastes like. Wondering what she feels like.

I need to stop this right now.

Andi doesn't need a horn-dog soccer player trying to get into her pants. She needs a friend to check on her just to make sure she's okay.

I can be that friend. It might kill me, but I can do it.

The next two days are carbon copies, with the exception of Andi trying to sniff me. I stay far enough away from her that she's not tempted. Or maybe it's because I don't think I'm strong enough to resist her temptation.

And at least once a night, she tells me she hates me, but from the twinkle in her eyes, I can tell she doesn't mean it. At least not anymore.

"You know, I really think I'm fine now. I haven't had a headache since yesterday. Surely, I'm out of the danger zone. Or at least the zone where I need a babysitter."

"I'm not your babysitter. I'm just a fr—"

Andi quickly puts a finger over my lips, preventing me from finishing my sentence. "Don't. We're not friends. We can't be friends. It's a conflict of interest."

I hold still, knowing if I move a muscle, it would be to take her finger in my mouth. I'm guessing she won't like that. Or more likely, she will, and that will be even worse. Then slowly, very slowly, she starts to trace the outline of my lips with a delicate touch.

Holy fuck, I could come from just that.

I stare into her blue eyes. We both feel the shift in the air. I snake one of my hands up to the back of her neck. I lean in and lower my lips to hers. They're warm and inviting, tasting like cinnamon and home. After a few moments of intermingled tongues and breath, I pull back. If I don't stop now, I don't know if I'll ever be able to.

"What changed for you?" I ask, my words coming in staccato pants.

"You're not who I thought you were."

What does she mean by that? "I'm exactly who I say I am. I don't pretend to be anything I'm not."

"You don't pretend, but you hide."

I pull back a little. "I'm out in the open on everything. I say what I think, pretty much at all times."

"You hide behind that persona so no one gets to know the real you."

Now I take a step back. Then another one. "That's bullshit. This is me. If you don't like it, leave it."

"You're in my place. You're the one who should leave." She folds her arms across her chest, eyes blazing.

"You're right, I should. And I will." I'm across her small floor in about three steps. I turn back to take one final look at her when I see the pattern of my red hair tie peeping through the messy blonde knot on the top of her head.

Damn, why is that so sexy?

One look at her face tells me she's not in the mood for any more frisky business, so I mentally tell my dick to calm down.

It works about as well as telling someone in the middle of a panic attack to calm down.

It doesn't matter though. Even if we wanted it to, this would never work. That thought makes me pause. But what if I wanted it to work?

What if *we* wanted it to work?

There's definitely something between us. No one gets me riled up like she does. What if I walk out of here and blow the only chance I will ever have with this woman?

Why am I thinking about this? As if I'll ever get the chance to put my mouth on hers again. As if this were a long-term thing.

As if there were feelings involved here.

"But what if ..." I say quietly, "what if we wanted to see what there is here between us? Because you know it's something."

She shakes her head. Her closed-off expression is back.

"Why not, Andi?"

"First of all, I hate you." Andi holds up a finger to count off her points. "Second of all," she continues, "this is going to cost me my career. The rumor of this"—she gestures between us—"was enough to have me scheduled to fly to Atlanta this week to meet with my supervisors. The *mere rumor*. And now? What am I supposed to say?"

"That we are two consenting adults who like the way each other smells and tastes."

She shakes her head, the frustration evident once again. "What am I supposed to do if I—by some huge stroke of luck—keep my job and have to officiate one of your games?"

"Don't give me a red card?"

Andi lets out a strangled scream. "Don't you see? You just screwed my career. How am I ever supposed to ref in the MUSSL again? This is a fireable offense."

"For you or for me?" Before this moment, I never considered that. Hell, I didn't even consider what it would mean for Andi. I just saw something I wanted, and I went for it. She touched me first.

It was just a kiss.

"Oh, come on, there's no way you'd even come close to being fired. They'd probably hang up a plaque for you in the locker room. You have no idea, do you? No idea what it's like for a woman in sports. Not only do women athletes get paid less than their male counterparts, but I as a referee get paid less to officiate a woman's game. And not only that, I get paid less than my male counterparts doing the same exact job. And for the same work at a lower rate, I get to deal with heckling, wolf whistles, and constant criticism that I don't know what I'm doing. Calls to go 'back to the kitchen where I belong.' Do you have to face any of that?"

We both know the answer, so I don't patronize her with one.

I do offer this, "If Mike Barnaby had made the same call you did, I would have yelled in his face too. I didn't get in your face because you're a woman. It's just what I do."

"Well, what you do set in motion a chain of events that has fucked me over. I think you and your stupid hair need to leave now."

I stare at her for a brief moment and then walk out the door without saying a word. I've never heard her curse like that. I get her point, I really do, but why'd she have to insult my hair?

As soon as the door shuts behind me, I open it back up. Andi looks up, startled over my quick return. "For the record, the reason I fouled Trevyon was because he was talking shit to me all game."

"Everyone talks shit," she fires back. "You need to have a thicker skin. If you're going to dish it out, you should be able to take it."

I shake my head. "No, he was talking shit about my sister. About how she was basically a crack whore and would do anything—and I mean anything—to get money for drugs. And that does include screwing Trevyon and a bunch of his friends when we were playing in Vegas. That's why I went after him. So yes, my behavior set about a chain of events, but I don't regret it. I don't care about many people in this world, but for those I do, I'll do anything."

And then I leave. For real this time.

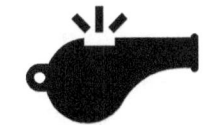

CHAPTER 30: ANDI

That was the stupidest thing I've ever done. Hands down. And that includes marrying Mike and attempting to dye my blonde hair black with box dye.

Those two things pale in comparison to kissing Brandon Nix.

Why? Why did I do it?

I've been asking myself the same question for two days.

I feel like shit, both emotionally and physically. Concussion recovery is no joke.

Not like my career is. I'll be the laughingstock of the sports world. First female to be the head referee in an official Men's United States Soccer League Game?

Andrea Nichols.

First female referee to get fired for making out with a player a few weeks later?

Andrea Nichols.

What the hell was I thinking?

As I lie in bed, staring at the ceiling, I know exactly what I was thinking. He saw me. He took care of me when I was injured. He didn't make me be quiet. He pushed me to talk and to have feelings.

I mean, I always have them, but no one cares. My feelings aren't important in the grand scheme of things. I'm so out of practice of having feelings that the minute they rise to the surface, they take over and make me do questionable things.

I'm better off not having feelings.

Or at least not expressing them.

Also, Brandon's sexy as hell.

Even with the debatable follicular choices, everything about him makes me want to do very bad things with him.

But what I can't stop thinking about is what Brandon said as he was leaving. That he only went after Trevyon Wallis-Smalls because of his sister. He was defending his sister.

That almost makes this all worth it.

I'd rather have a man that protects his family than one who lets someone sling insults. Not that I *have* Brandon. Or that I ever will. Just … it makes me feel all sorts of gushy inside.

There are so many feelings swirling inside me that I barely know which way is up.

Nathan postponed my meeting, thanks to my concussion. I almost wish he hadn't. No use in prolonging the inevitable. The Global Games are over and the MUSSL resumes regulation play next week.

Even without the knowledge that we have been fraternizing outside of work, I doubt Nathan will put me on another game.

It's probably better that way.

Maybe he'll keep me in the WUSSL, working at a lower rate for a lower-rated league. If I stay officiating games in the WUSSL, I'll never be able to quit my day job.

I don't know why I'm still thinking about this in terms of a viable career path.

Maybe because refereeing was the one thing I got to do that was on my terms. I couldn't play soccer at a competitive level because my family couldn't make that kind of commitment. I went to PT school because of Benj. Made sense, right? Therapy had been such a big part of his life that I should give back on his behalf. Pivoting into refereeing started as a hobby when I was in college and took off from there.

I did it for me.

It's one of the few things I ever did for myself.

Even if I did throw my career away with both hands, I still made history. I should be proud of that.

I haul myself out of bed. To do what? I'm not exactly sure. I have three more days before I'm expected to log back into my soul-sucking day job. If I could, I'd break every single fragile item in my apartment. Even then, I'm not sure it would help.

But I bet it would feel awesome.

It's probably beyond what I'm supposed to do, but in all reality, I feel fine. I could have gone back to work today, but I decided to take the entire week. It's been three days since I kissed Brandon.

Not that I'm counting or anything.

I haven't heard from him.

Not that I expected to. Especially not with the things I said to him.

Want to know the funny thing? I don't even have a way to get ahold of him. We never exchanged numbers or anything. He's been in my place more than anyone else, and I can't even text him.

Not that I would.

Or that I want to.

I mean, I think I'd feel a little better if I could at least apologize for the comments about his hair. Those were uncalled for.

My phone dings. I don't race to see who it is. There are only three likely possibilities: Benj, Mike, or Nathan. I don't want to talk to any of them.

I'm still mad at Benj for freezing me out and not telling me about Samantha or his plans. Maybe mad isn't the right word? Maybe it's hurt that I'm so invisible to him too that he forgot I was supposed to be important to him.

I never want to talk to Mike these days. Everything about him grates on me. But mostly because he gets paid more for doing the same exact job I do. And he knows it too. Yet he's not doing anything to speak up for me.

Though you can bet if the situation was reversed, he'd be begging me to go to the mat for him.

I don't think I need to explain why I don't want to talk to Nathan. The longer I go without hearing from him, the more I can be delusional that no one will ever find out, and I'll get to keep my job.

If that should happen, I know I could be super professional in a Buzzards' game. I could be impartial and fair. Nobody would believe it though.

Finally, my curiosity gets the better of me. It's Hannah LaRosa.

Hannah: You okay?

Why is she texting me that? Am I viral again? Has someone posted Brandon coming and going from my place? I quickly open ClikClak and search around. There's nothing about Brandon or me.

Hannah herself has plenty to use, if she wanted. She doesn't seem like the type. In fact, she seems like the type of person I might be able to someday call a friend.

Me: Okay. Why?

Hannah: Cally said you had a concussion

Relief floods my body. She doesn't know.

Me: Yeah. I'm okay. It was minor. Feeling back to my old self. But don't tell my day job that. I told them I needed the whole week off.

Hannah: Your secret is safe with me

I suck in a deep breath. What does she mean by that?

Me: I hope they all are

Hannah doesn't keep me in suspense.

Hannah: Of course. The whole thing is ridiculous. Just because you are both passionate and intense does not mean there's anything going on between you. Society is stupid sometimes.

While I agree with her, I don't respond. I don't want to lie to her, but it's also obvious she doesn't know. That's a relief.

A small one, but a relief nonetheless.

My relief is short-lived when I get a message from Sydney requesting I login for a Zoom call with Nathan in 10 minutes. I jump out of bed, run to the bathroom, and brush both my teeth and my hair. I'm not sure why I brush my teeth. It's not like Nathan will smell my breath through the computer screen. On the other hand, I've been shirking my self-care this week, so they're in desperate need of brushing regardless.

I put on a non-stained T-shirt. That's about as good as it's going to get before it's time to log in. I haven't been at my computer all week, and I have to say, it's felt good.

"Hello, Andi," Nathan greets.

"Hi, Nathan. Sorry about the game this week. This is the first time I've been out of bed in days." Not for the reason you think, but self-loathing feels just about as bad as a concussion does.

"I need to speak with you about a delicate matter."

Shit. Here it comes. My hands grasp the edge of my chair until my knuckles ache with exertion.

"Okay." I keep my face still, my expression unreadable.

"Leora Deventhorpe reached out to Sydney."

While the name sounds vaguely familiar, I can't place it, so I sit there, unmoving.

"She is in the public relations department with the Boston Buzzards."

Oh God, it's happening. I don't know what I'm going to say in my defense. I'll have to fess up. If he asks, I'll admit it.

"The Buzzards are working with an organization called ..." He looks down and I hear papers shuffling. "JustSibs. They're doing a soccer clinic prior to a game."

Relief pours through my body like a dam breaking.

"Are you familiar with the organization?" he asks.

I nod slightly. My neck feels stiff. "Yes. I believe they work under another organization, but I can't remember the name right now. My memory is a little fuzzy because of the concussion. JustSibs helps to support kids and teens with chronically ill siblings. I was looking at working with them because my brother has a form of muscular dystrophy. While I appreciated all the things the MDA and Make a Wish did for my brother, there was never really much to support me."

There's a long pause. "Ah, that makes sense now. Leora Deventhorpe asked if we could have some referees there before the game on September first to work on this event. She asked for you, specifically."

Now I grip the sides of my chair to hold myself up. It takes every ounce of strength I have not to sag with relief.

"I wanted to check with you before I committed you to this event. We'll go ahead and change your schedule around and put you on for the Buzzards–

Wave match later that day. That'll mean we have to take you off of two WUSSL matches due to conflicts. Are you okay with that?"

"Of course." Nathan's writing something down, and I can see his attention isn't really on me. Since luck is on my side today, I decide to try one more thing. "I'm happy to help and be flexible," I say with a smile, as if Nathan hasn't been giving me the runaround about absolute bullshit for weeks. "One more thing. I need to check with payroll because it seems there's been a clerical error. Do you have the pay schedule and rates for both the MUSSL and WUSSL games? I only need the ones for Level 3."

Nathan's still writing. "Do you want the men's or the women's tables?" he asks absent-mindedly before his head jerks up. "I meant the ones for the men's league or the women's league?"

Gotcha.

Sweetly I smile as I say, "I'll take them all. Thanks so much! Let me know about the JustSibs thing. I'm happy to represent the USSLRA at such a meaningful event."

I'm about to exhale a sigh of relief when Nathan suddenly narrows his gaze. "Is there anything you want to tell me about your involvement with the Boston Buzzards? Brandon Nix specifically?"

I know I'm going to hell for lying, but I have to try. "Actually, yes."

This has his full attention.

I continue. "Brandon and I both have an interest in this charity. I have a disabled brother, and he has a sister who also has required a fair amount of care.

This organization means a lot to the both of us. We'd both been in contact with JustSibs, and they asked us to work together to plan some activities. But that's it. That's why we've met on two occasions, to attempt to put our differences aside on behalf of this charity. We just both want to help siblings who are going through a lot. We realized how this could look, which is why we are going through our official channels."

Nathan nods. "As long as nothing else is going on."

I smile. "Nathan, how long have you known me? Do you really think I'd jeopardize everything for someone like Brandon Nix? I live for refereeing. You know that. This cause is about the only reason you'll even catch me within a 500-yard radius of that man outside of game days."

The best part about having to hide my expressions for my entire life is that no one knows how to read me. It makes me a convincing liar. Nathan buys it hook, line, and sinker. I might get away with this.

Now all I have to do is work one stupid charity event with Brandon, and I'm off the hook.

I just need to never think about kissing him—or more—again.

That's easy.

CHAPTER 31: BRANDON

My days are spent in a whirlwind of workouts, practices, and working with Leora on the event. We're calling it Soccer for Sibs. I've recruited several of my teammates to work. We have a game that evening against the Miami Wave, so everyone will be around anyway.

I'm also spending a fair amount of time working with Watson Ross. This will come as a total shock—I know it did to me—but I have a lot to unpack. If we start with the surface problem of my sister, being the sibling of an addict causes significant trauma. It's not dissimilar to some of the wounds that having a sick sibling cause.

On that front, my sister is actually doing well for once. Jess texts me every other day when she goes into town, where she has reception. If she's not going to make it to be able to text me, she lets me know ahead of time. I never realized how much energy I expended worrying about Jess.

It's not like I don't worry now, but it's much less than it used to be. It's not accompanied by this overwhelming sense of dread each time my phone rings.

"I want you to consider your public persona. How you act around others. What's that about?" Ross asks me.

I shrug. "I tell it like it is."

"Why?" he prods.

"I don't like liars or fakes. It's probably because of my sister."

"Were you this outspoken before the accident?"

I normally try to avoid thinking about that period of my life at all costs. Hell, I think I've repressed a fair amount of it. I think about what my coaches said about me. The comments that were made during the academy.

Needs to be more confident.

Needs to attack the ball with purpose.

Lacks aggression when taking possession.

Skilled but timid.

Ha! I showed them.

Or did I?

"Would it surprise you to know that anger, aggression, and oppositional behaviors are all commonly seen in siblings of sick children?"

"Jess wasn't sick. Not the way And—" I catch myself. "Not the way the kids at the event are. I mean their siblings. Plus, it's not like we were kids. I was 18. Jess was 16. I was an adult."

"Neither of you had a fully developed frontal cortex. Plus, not only did Jess become an addict, but you also lost your mom too. You experienced massive trauma. You've emotionally stalled out at the age you were at the time of the accident."

His point *may* have some merit, but I'm not ready to accept it yet. I grasp at the statement that's been my reality for the past 14 years.

"If it hadn't been for me, none of it would have happened in the first place." This is the first time I have admitted it out loud. My dad's told me it plenty of times, but until this moment, I didn't realize I really believed it. I look up at Ross, trying to make sense of what's happening.

"It's counterproductive to have thoughts like that. You were not responsible for the actions of another. You weren't the one drunk driving. Even your sister, who was driving, wasn't at fault. Only one person was responsible for the tragic actions of that day."

"Yeah but—"

"No 'yeah buts.' That is the truth. Don't hold onto something that isn't yours. Don't carry that bag of rocks for no reason. It's weighing you down."

I sit there for a minute, processing.

"And if I didn't make it abundantly clear, I believe your aggression and attitude is a trauma response. It's a defense mechanism. Work through that trauma, and your attitude should fix itself."

I look at Watson Ross skeptically. He holds up his hands sheepishly. "Okay, not fix itself, but it will be easier to respond in a less over-the-top way."

That makes more sense.

I leave the appointment with an overwhelming desire to call Andi. To be perfectly clear, I've never *ever* had the desire to call a woman for anything other than a booty call. I want to tell her what I'm learning in therapy.

I wonder if she's ever gone to therapy.

It might help.

Maybe she has, because what she said to me is not that dissimilar to what Watson Ross just said.

I can't call her though, because I don't have her number. I suppose I could message her on ClikClak, but that seems weird. What am I supposed to say?

How are you feeling? I want to kiss you again. You should totally check out therapy.

Yeah, maybe I'm not ready to reach out. But I can't stop thinking about her. How she felt for those brief moments in my arms. How her mouth tasted. How I didn't feel like I had anything to prove with her.

I need to let it go. Next session, I'll ask Watson Ross about that. He's got to have some ideas for getting over someone who was never into you in the first place.

Leora calls me into the office after practice. "In addition to you, Callaghan and Landon will be at the event. We're hoping to have four stations of players set up, so can you ask one more of your teammates?"

"Why can't you ask them?" I'm not the asking-a-favor type.

"Because this is your show. You wanted to do this event, you can take an active role in it."

I start to make a snide comment about her attitude, but I catch myself. Maybe she's having a bad day for a reason I know nothing about. Maybe she's just reflecting the attitude I've given to the club over the years. Maybe the elastic on her underwear is shot, and it's stressing her out.

I may never know, but I can temper how I react.

Jesus, this therapy thing is working.

"Sure. I'll ask around. When do you need the name?"

Leora is already typing away on her keyboard. She doesn't even look up as she says, "Yesterday. The newsletters and flyers have to go out."

I walk out and run promptly into TJ Doyle. He's a total social media whore, so he'd be perfect for this type of thing. "Hey, Doyle, wanna do a publicity event? It's for charity, but there'll be tons of photo ops."

He's got the biggest ClikClak following of any of us, so I know, if for no other reason, he'll do it. He doesn't miss a chance to post about his perfectly manicured life.

"Yeah, sure."

I fill him in on the details and promptly return to tell Leora that TJ will be our fourth. Four stations. Not five. There isn't a referee involved.

Andi's not doing the event.

It shouldn't surprise me. She made it pretty clear when she kicked me out that I'd ruined her life. For the record, she was an equal—and enthusiastic—participant. I guess I'm to blame for being so totally irresistible that she couldn't keep her hands off me.

It's a curse.

In the back of my mind, I thought I'd see Andi at the Soccer for Sibs event. I was holding out hope.

That says a lot. I'm not a man who hopes for much.

I google her name to see if there's been anything about her getting fired. There isn't. She's still on the USSLRA website as staff. So it's not a job thing. She isn't going to be there because she doesn't want to see me.

I'd rather take a spike to the nuts than feel how this makes me feel.

CHAPTER 32: ANDI

I got away with it.

It's been over a month and no one is the wiser.

Nathan has no idea what went down between Brandon and me. For the past four plus weeks, I've been meticulously scouring social media. I guess it's true—out of sight, out of mind. For someone desperate for attention, that's a bad thing.

I love it.

Not that I almost threw out my career for a man, but that the world seems to have forgotten that I exist.

My whole life has been spent flying under the radar. Being in the background. Not taking up space. Not being seen. I don't know how to function otherwise.

Brandon Nix is exhibit A.

He put me in the center of his focus for two days, and I practically climbed that man like a tree.

I will until the end of time insist that it was because of the concussion. Yet deep down, I know it wasn't.

I wanted him.

I wanted to kiss him.

Truth be told, I would have done more.

He made me feel valued and like I was the center of his world for a few minutes. I didn't know how much I needed to feel that from someone. Never in a million years did I think that someone would be Brandon Nix.

It doesn't matter.

It can never be again. I dodged a huge bullet on this. Let's face it, I deserve to get fired. At least now I do. I mean, this situation is almost comical. The way this whole damn thing has played out. I would never have been with Brandon if I wasn't trying to prove I wasn't with Brandon.

Just saying that statement makes my head spin.

But it's true. My mere existence as a woman put me under a microscope which set a chain of events in motion. When the accusations of fraternization started, there was definitely nothing going on between Brandon and me. So maybe I deserve my punishment now, but at least I finally did something to earn it.

At least if I get fired now, I'll know what it felt like to have his lips on mine.

I should probably disclose this to Nathan as soon as possible.

It also means I'll never officiate a men's game again.

Lots of people do shady things and get away with it. I can still work this game and be fair. I'm not the head official. I'm scheduled to be the assistant for the game. Mike—unfortunately—will be the referee for the Wave vs. Buzzards. The game will not be in my hands. Mike will be in charge of the lion's share of the calls.

I can be fair, even if I am a liar.

Mike calls me the night before the Soccer for Sibs event. "Wanna ride together tomorrow? You know, for old time's sake?"

Ew, no. I have less tolerance for my ex-husband than ever. Brandon did more for me in four days than Mike did in two years. I was there for Mike, but I can honestly say the feeling wasn't mutual. It was just as much my fault as Mike's. I let it happen.

Like I've let most of my life happen.

Maybe I need to be a little more like Brandon.

I mean, not the rude, spluttering, Neanderthal parts, but the parts where he speaks up when there's something that should be said.

You know, like when I'm not getting paid enough.

"I have to be down to Foxboro for 10 a.m., so I was planning on leaving by nine at the latest. How early are you going down?" I know damn well Mike won't get to the game until the last possible minute. If I ever walked in right when I was supposed to, I'd be criticized for being late. No one blinks an eye when any male ref shows up right before it's time to take the field.

Also, have I mentioned I hate running late?

"Ten? The game's not until six. I didn't plan on leaving until about four. Why so early? I mean, you've always been a little neurotic about being on time, but this is pushing it."

I hold both middle fingers up in a silent salute to the man I cannot believe I married. Maybe next time I see him, I'll do that to him in person. "There's a charity event I'm appearing at before the game. It's at the Buzzards' practice facility."

Mike scoffs. "Why'd they ask you? Nobody asked me to go." The tone of his voice clearly indicates he's hurt. He's always had a fragile ego that needed lots of fluffing. He's definitely a *pick me* type.

Also, he still cannot get it through his piddly brain that people value me and my work. I'm not his wife anymore, so it's no longer my job to explain my worth. As long as I know it, that's all that matters. Instead, I explain the premise of the event to him.

"Yeah, but why'd they pick you? I'm the head official for the game. It would make sense for me to be at the clinic."

Mike only met Benj in person once or twice during the time we were together. Of course, one of those was *at* our wedding. I still talked to—and about—my brother all the time. The fact that Mike can so easily forget the person who means the most to me makes my blood boil.

"Maybe because I'm just like the kids who will be attending. I grew up with a sick sibling. I can relate to them."

Mike laughs. "Andi, you can't relate to anyone. You're too much of a machine. You don't even like kids. It's why we never had any."

Normally, my reaction to Mike would be to say something banal and placating, end the phone conversation as soon as possible, and then ruminate about it for months.

However, I don't even know what normal is for me anymore. "Actually, Mike, for the record, I don't have a problem with kids. What I do have a problem with is sacrificing my body to carry them when I'm already pushing myself to the peak of my performance levels just to do my job. Because my job—the thing I want most in the world—won't cut me any slack for growing a human being. Instead, it would penalize my time off, thereby impacting my ability to be promoted to the next level. You would not have been forced to diminish your training or take time off. Your career would not have changed at all. And that's just the pregnancy. How would we have ever raised a child working the schedules we worked? We could barely take vacations or even date nights. It would have meant the end of my career for me, and I wasn't ready to give it up, certainly not for you."

Then I disconnect.

It feels good to hang up on Mike.

It feels good to feel.

I pick up the phone and call him back. I don't wait for him to say anything before launching in again.

"And another thing, it's ass that you get paid more for doing the same job and you know it and you haven't said anything."

"That's why it would have made sense for you to take time off with the baby. The loss of my salary would have impacted us more."

THIS IS THE ARGUMENT HE MAKES?

"I'm not even going to dignify that with a response. It's a moot point now. We didn't have kids because I didn't want them with you. You're not a good partner because you don't see me as equal. You never have and you never will. I'll see you at the game."

I hang up for a second time.

We didn't even fight like that when we were getting divorced. He told me I was boring and that I didn't have a personality. He was also screwing a secretary at the USSLRA office.

Somehow, that didn't endanger his career.

If anything, it made him more masculine and virile, which automatically made him more qualified to do his job.

It's bullshit.

It's in the past.

I don't know what my future holds, except there's no place for Mike in it. I've wasted enough time and energy on him.

It's time to prepare not only for the game but the clinic tomorrow.

The more I look into JustSibs and their website, Coping Space, the more I'm learning about the effect growing up with Benj had on me. I wouldn't change it for the world. I love my brother most of all. But I wish I knew how to love him without diminishing myself.

It's a pattern I seem to be repeating.

I didn't think there was enough time, love, and attention to go around. Benj obviously needed more than I did. But that didn't mean I didn't have any needs myself.

And aside from showing these kids at the clinic the very best time ever, I have one more thing I desperately need.

Equal pay for equal work.

The morning of the clinic is here. I barely slept at all, thinking about the day to come. No problem, I can handle this.

I can handle anything.

Until I walk into the Boston Buzzards training facility and see Brandon Nix standing there.

My step falters before I regain my footing. The last time I stumbled because of Brandon I ended up with a mild brain injury, and we all know what happened next. I don't think the outside observer would notice my slight loss of rhythm. Nor would they see the lump forming in my throat or the tightness constricting my chest.

He looks good.

His hair is slicked back into a low ponytail. It looks shorter than before. There's not as much blond on the ends. His normal five o'clock shadow has grown in thicker, almost to a full beard at this point. He's wearing his glasses.

Damn.

I love those glasses.

Brandon's joking around with his teammates, bouncing a soccer ball on his knees.

I've been around soccer players my entire life. I've played soccer since I was a kid. Until the COVID pandemic, I played in a few recreational leagues. I'm not usually impressed with this type of horsing around.

Is it hot in here or is it his thighs?

I swallow, allowing myself one more look before I shut all those feelings away. I can't have them. I can't think them. They cannot exist.

It's probably a good thing I've had a lifetime's worth of experience not allowing myself to feel or express anything. I'm going to need every single bit of it today.

CHAPTER 33: BRANDON

She's here.

The minute she walks into the field house that serves as our practice field, my eyes find her. She looks good. Her hair is in a high ponytail, swirling and bouncing with each step.

I want to grab it and pull her toward me.

I can't. I will never be able to do that, and I have to accept that.

I want to know what she's been up to this past month. How is she feeling? Did she ever get the pay thing straightened out?

I'm probably too loud, talking with my teammates. I'm probably showing off too much, messing around with the ball. I don't know what to do with myself or my energy that isn't running over to her and scooping her into my arms.

I did not for one second anticipate it would be this difficult to see her again.

It's heaven and hell all rolled into one.

My new-found self-consciousness is a real pain in the ass. Reprieve arrives in the form of the event organizers who begin to herd us into our designated corners. "Remember, today is about the siblings. Do what you can to make them feel special. We expect lots of social media posts, so make sure to smile big. Thank you for donating your time and names to this event today."

I feel eyes on me, especially from Leora and Callaghan. Hannah is here, filming away.

I pose for her, and she laughs. "You gonna work for us now? Do our social media?"

It's Hannah's turn to laugh. "You know it's best to keep some separation between work and home. I'm happy with where I'm at. The networking is good. If I'd thought about it, I'd have brought some of my football players over." Since Hannah's now running social media and other public relations for the Patriots, she could have.

"You should have brought your guys over. I'd show them how to really kick a ball."

Hannah laughs. "Oh, to have your confidence. We should have you put your money where your mouth is."

TJ Doyle walks up, holding his phone out, obviously filming. "What's Brandon talking smack about now? I want to record this for posterity."

"You want to go viral at my expense."

Doyle laughs. "Same difference. What's the bet?"

I look at Hannah. This is all in good fun. "That I can kick a ball further than the kicker for the Patriots. Bring him over. We should do this. Get Chris Todd and let's have a kickoff contest. I've got time before the game."

Callaghan walks up, catching the end of the conversation. "Sounds like it'd be worth watching, but not on a match day. Save your leg for the game, especially in this heat."

"Cally Entay is always spoiling the fun," I pretend to pout, mugging for Doyle. I know Entay hates that nickname. I may be trying to be better, but I can't let everything go.

The next ninety minutes are a whirlwind. Kids of all ages line up at my station. I'm at the back of the practice field, teaching penalty kicks. Entay's working on goalkeeping skills. Doyle and Landon are working on passing and other drills. Periodically a buzzer rings and the entire group rotates to the next station.

Andi's at the opposite end of the field from me. It's good she's far away. It's bad that she's in my line of sight. What's she saying down there? She's all smiles, hugging kid after kid.

Her expression is easy to read, even from this far away.

She looks happy.

Andi Nichols is a natural in this environment. She laughs as kid after kid pulls out a red card and holds it up. Each kid at her station gets a whistle as well.

That's great, said no one ever.

As the event draws to a conclusion, we gather at midfield for lots of group pictures. We're all wearing matching T-shirts and smiles. The participants are ushered out the door, and the rest of us are left to take some last photos with the organizers of the event.

Through no fault of my own or any underlying agenda, I end up next to Andi. She gives me a slight lift of her chin but no other acknowledgment. She's not slighting me. This is how it needs to be.

It feels like a slight.

Nothing can ever happen with her again. No matter how many times I've thought about it. No matter how many times I've wanted to call her. No matter what I want.

Being with her would ruin her life, and I can't do that to her.

I won't do that to her.

"Get in closer so you all fit behind the side. Turn a little sideways." The photographer waves at us. "You on the end, get a little closer."

As directed, I take a step in toward Andi. There are only inches between our bodies. This is hell, not being able to touch her. In front of me, her posture is rigid. I can see the pulse thrumming in her neck. She swallows hard.

Good.

I mean, not good because this is agony and there's nothing we can do about it. But good that I affect her. Because even if I were to confront her—even if she denied it—her body doesn't lie.

It's written all over her.

I can read her like a book, and that book wants to be open to me.

That'll have to be enough for me.

My self-control isn't that good. At the last moment, I stretch out my hand, my fingers grazing hers. We're so close that this could look like an incidental brushing. For a split second, her fingers curl into mine.

It's all the confirmation I need. This is hell for her too.

The moment the pictures are done, she all but sprints out of there. Part of me understands. She can't be caught fraternizing with the team she's about to officiate. She can't be caught fraternizing with *me*.

Slowly I walk behind my teammates to the locker room where I'd pitched my bag upon arrival. I strip off my long socks and shin guards, sliding my feet into my flip-flops. I have time to run home for a quick shower and lunch before I need to report back for the game.

I wonder what Andi's going to do with this downtime. There's not enough time for her to drive home and back. It's probably a good thing I don't have her number. I don't have the willpower not to text her and offer to let her shower at my house. With me.

I said I'm working on being a good person. I'm not one yet.

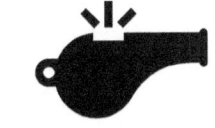

CHAPTER 34: ANDI

Thank goodness for long cold showers.

Mostly because it's 85 degrees with oppressive humidity, and it's only early afternoon. Also because standing next to Brandon Nix sets my body on fire. My fingers still burn where he touched me.

As the water sluices over me, I think about the saltwater fish tank my dad bought for Benj and me right after we'd moved to Colorado. It was super cool, and Benj and I used to sit in front of it for hours and watch the fish and other reef dwellers who called our 35-gallon tank home. He'd bought something called live rock from the aquarium supply store. It looked like big pieces of rock with a lot of holes in it. Nothing special. Certainly nothing exciting. As time went on, more and more critters and creatures emerged from the rock. It really was alive.

This was before the internet, so I used to have to go to the library and get books out to look up what I was seeing to identify it. Eventually, Benj and I were able to label all the residents of our tank. There were tons of limpets, some snails, and even a crab that emerged. We had Aiptasia, of course, which is an invasive and problematic type of anemone. My dad was looking up how to kill those, but I thought they were pretty. Hands down, the coolest thing to come out of the rock was a spiny sea urchin.

Benj and I named him Spike.

Spike was super active, moving around the tank on a daily basis. My dad liked him because he ate algae. Benj and I liked him because he was entertaining. All in all, Spike was an unexpected, added bonus to our lives. Until the morning I came out to find the water in the tank cloudy and every single creature—fish and invertebrates alike—dead. Spike included, lying on the sandy gravel at the bottom of the tank, his oral surface facing up. Spike was right underneath the heater, which had a hole in it.

He'd eaten it, causing the heater to malfunction and raise the water temperature from a balmy 78 degrees to over 100. He'd boiled them all alive.

That's how being around Brandon Nix makes me feel. Like I'm boiling alive. Maybe that's why he has an ice bath.

Spike is the perfect analogy for Brandon. That should be his spirit animal. Comes out of nowhere, looks poisonous, is actually pretty cool and entertaining, kills you in the end.

Yes, definitely Brandon's spirit animal.

And if Brandon is Spike, I'm the live rock. I look dead on the surface, but in reality, there are a lot of living things within me, waiting to emerge. But as these feelings, wants, and needs emerge, I'm finding it harder and harder to keep my poker face.

If I'm not careful, I'm going to die because of Brandon.

Not actually, but my career—and maybe my heart—will.

Shit. That's the first time thinking of Brandon has made me think of my heart and feelings.

Oh no, this is not good. Not good at all.

I emerge from the shower, skin pruny and my mind even less at ease. Officiating the game today is not going to be as easy as I'd thought. I deserve this anguish. I played with fire, so I deserve to get burned. Wrapped in my towel, I dash to my bag to extract my clothes. This may be the referees' private locker room, but I'm still sharing it with a team of three men. None of them are here yet, though I expect them to start trickling in any minute.

The last thing I need is for rumors to start about me being naked in the presence of my colleagues.

I don't need rumors about sleeping my way to the top to surface.

I add the locker room situation to a long list of things I need to discuss with my union representative. We have a phone call set for Monday morning. I can't let this wage thing go on any longer.

I pull on my underwear and sports bra, and then my black regulation shorts. I comb through my wet hair and let it fan out on my shoulders. I'll put it up before the game. Sitting down, I eat my pre-game meal. I always bring the same thing: yogurt, two hard boiled eggs for protein, fruit, and rice cakes. I've got a fruit smoothie for right before the game as well as water and electrolyte drinks.

I don't get stoppage time if I have a cramp from dehydration.

Hell, my entire leg could be falling off, and I'd never request they stop the game for me. It would only mean more ridicule and criticism about how females aren't capable of performing at this level. If I'm prepared, I can prevent things like cramps and running out of gas from happening.

This is the fuel my body needs.

Mentally, I want to bury my face in a dozen donuts or a gallon of vodka. If I didn't think it would make me vomit on the sidelines, I'd be inhaling a pint of Ben and Jerry's right about now. How could I be so stupid as to think that I'd be fine with all this? How could I not realize that all those spicy dreams I've been having over the last several weeks—all starring Brandon, naturally—were not just a coincidence? It wasn't simply because he was on my mind.

Oh no, my body was trying to get it through my brain that there was something she wanted. My brain's always been the one to shut down. To push all my feelings into deep, dark corners where they all but disappeared. As long as the light doesn't shine upon them, they don't exist.

Something won't let Brandon retreat to the dark for me.

My limpets and snails are out, and there's no crawling back in the rock for me.

Okay, I really need to come up with a better analogy.

I'm sure today will be challenging, but I'll get through it. Just like I do everything else. This is simply a minor inconvenience. It's not like I'm going to die if I can't ever touch Brandon again. If I can't see him smile at me. If I can't feel his lips on mine. It won't kill me.

It just feels that way right now.

For right now, I have a job to do. Once this game is over, I'm going to give myself permission to feel a little sad for a few days. I don't have much time to wallow. I hear voices coming down the hall. Quickly, I pull my shirt over my head and pick up my food containers.

Rico Lopez and Hamilton Regan enter the room, laughing casually. They both stop when they see me. They don't need to say a word to let me know I'm not one of them.

It's fine.

I mean, it's not, but that's why I'll be talking to my union in two days' time. Maybe something will get better.

We all have our own rituals for pre-game prep. I've reviewed footage from the teams and looked at their stats. I put my shin guards in and pull up my long black socks before tightly lacing and tying my cleats. Then it's time to brush my hair back into a tight ponytail. Because of the heat and humidity today, I add a cloth headband to slick back flyaways.

In a few minutes, I'll go out and walk the field. We're all responsible for inspecting the players to make sure they're wearing proper equipment and not wearing anything illegal, like watches or jewelry, so we'll do that as a group.

Generally, it's the head referee's job to inspect the condition of the pitch and the goals, but since Mike isn't here, I want to look for myself. Something on the field, especially the sidelines where I'll be running back and forth as the assistant, can be dangerous to the players as well as myself.

Because of the chilly environment in the locker room—and I don't mean the air conditioning—I head out to the field. Some of the kids from the Soccer for Sibs are running back and forth over the green grass, living out their soccer dreams. A few players from the Buzzards are out there with them.

Brandon's one of them.

Naturally, my gaze lands on him like gravity pulling me back to Earth. As quickly as I can manage, I look away. I see Bjorn Janssen on the sidelines, so I go to speak with him.

"Assistant today, Ms. Nichols?" he greets.

I nod. "Mike Barnaby will be out in a few." If he's even here yet. "The event earlier today was a lot of fun. Thank you for including me in it. I'm sure you know of the personal connection."

He smiles. "Yes. It was good of you to come as well. Too often, there are feelings of separation between players and officials."

"I know. People forget we're all here to create an entertaining game for the fans. I don't set out with any agendas." I don't want any hard feelings about the last game I officiated here. Nor do I want him to think I'm coming in with a preconceived notion about his team.

Or any players on his team.

Trust me, I have no idea how he's going to act.

"Most teams can say the same thing. Good luck to you." He steps away, having been summoned by a staff member on the field. I can't check the goals yet, but the condition of the field looks okay. It'll have to be checked once it's cleared, which should be any moment.

Plus, that's Mike's job, not mine. He's getting paid more. He should do more.

As Brandon trots back through the tunnel to the locker rooms, I finally start to calm down. This will be okay. I can do this. I'm here to do a job that I've worked too long and too hard to let anyone take away from me.

Let's do this.

CHAPTER 35: BRANDON

ndi holds the flag in her right hand. She raises it up and then out in front of her. Offsides. It's me. I'm the offender. I'm also totally offside, so I raise my hand sheepishly. Barnaby blows his whistle, and the Wave get their indirect penalty kick.

Considering we're in the second half, and I've amassed no direct penalties, fouls, or cards, I'd consider this a good game. It's practically one for the record books.

Not to mention I've already scored once from two yards outside the penalty area, which was probably about 35 yards or so, give or take. The majority of my goals are from this range. I wasn't kidding about challenging Chris Todd from the Patriots to a kickoff.

The Wave gets their ball down onto our half of the field. Cally scoops it up and launches it in a drop kick past the midline of the field. Midfielder

Merriweather Hayes traps the ball and, with one smooth motion, boots it across the field to me. I can see the shot as clear as day. I'm to the left of center, downfield enough to not seem like a threat. I make sure to watch the offsides this time, knowing Andi's trained eye is upon me.

She's not doing it to bust my balls. She's very good at what she does.

The ball arrives like a line drive right to me. With perfect timing, I take a step with my right foot, swinging my left back in preparation for contact. I'm more accurate with my right foot but can be dangerous with either one.

As I am right now.

My left foot makes contact and the ball sails into the upper corner of the goal. This one's 36 yards, from the opposite side of the field as the last one. Not too shabby for my "weaker" foot. I yell, striking my signature muscle arm pose before I run up to Landon, jumping on him as I do with every goal.

"That's two, man. Hat trick?" Jacob Pavlovic asks as we jog back to midfield to set up for Miami Wave's kickoff.

"I'll try. Set me up."

I'm running out of time for a hat trick, but it's all I can think about now. I haven't had one since May, so I'm due.

Today feels like the day.

It's also just basic math that you have a higher probability of scoring more if you don't have to leave the game because of penalties. I should remember that.

As the Wave pushes into our half of the field, we drop back in an attempt to regain control of the ball. We're up, three–nil, so the Wave is no longer pulling their punches in their attempt to score.

Quite literally.

Barnaby doesn't seem to be calling tons. Andi'd be blowing her whistle right and left. I glance over at her. Assistant referees can call from the sidelines, especially if the head referee misses them. It's a large field with lots of moving pieces. I feel like she sees most of it.

Xavier Henry, playing defense, pops the ball up the field. I see it coming and run toward it. I jump, trapping it with the inner portion of my thigh. As the ball hits the ground, I begin to dribble it. Just as I make it past the midfield mark, I feel a shove in the middle of my back, causing me to pitch forward and stumble. I roll on the ground for a moment before popping back up.

Barnaby blows his whistle, his arm directly out to the side. Direct free kick. He places the ball and signals to me. I'm just in front of the midfield line. While the opposing team is allowed to make a wall in front of me, I'm far enough out that there's not much of a threat.

I love it when people underestimate me.

It's a drill I've practiced for years. Two steps and kick.

The ball sails through the air and right over the hands of the Wave goalie for the third time today.

GOOOOAAAAAL!

I pump my arms, running toward my teammates. I jump on Landon. The crowd chants "Hat trick! Hat trick!" as they toss their caps onto the field. The officials have to stop to clear the field of any debris.

It's prolonging the inevitable, which is a crushing defeat of the Miami Wave. This has been one of the best, cleanest, games of my career. Hopefully it does something to help with my probationary status.

Coach Janssen signals me to see if I want to come out. Of course I don't, but it's also a good move to let another teammate who doesn't see as much playing time have their shot. The score is four–nothing with just over five minutes left plus stoppage time. I see Andy Bracer at half-field. With the next stoppage of play, I'll be out.

The ball moves toward the sideline. Maliq Miller and Seamus O'Marra battle for the ball. They run together, shoulder to shoulder, checking each other, fighting for control. Maliq kicks the ball which ricochets off O'Marra's foot and out of bounds. O'Marra stumbles, catapulting out of control and out of bounds as well.

Right into Andi.

She backpedals, attempting to keep her balance but can't with the velocity of O'Marra's body. They both fall to the ground.

I freeze for a second, unable to tear my eyes away from Andi. What if she hit her head again? Another concussion this soon could be devastating. Is she hurt? O'Marra hit her pretty hard. I want to run over and help her. To pull her to her feet and make sure she's okay. Instead, I drop my head for a second before heading to the sideline.

As I'm crossing the line, I glance again at Andi. O'Marra pulls her to her feet. In one smooth move, as soon as she's on her feet, O'Marra lets her go while reaching around and grabbing her ass, squeezing for a moment before letting go and walking away, a shit-eating grin on his face as he winks.

Her eyes are wide, mouth agape. Absolute shock is written all over her face.

No one touches her like that.

I immediately see her signaling for a red card. I also see that Mike Barnaby is ignoring her.

My mind goes red. I charge at Seamus O'Marra. He doesn't see me coming. He certainly doesn't see my fist cock back before it lands squarely on his jaw. "If you ever touch her like that again, I'll make you wish you were never born." We both land on the ground with a thud I barely register. I continue to hit until I feel myself being lifted off O'Marra.

My teammates physically restrain me as I yell a string of expletives that are sure to have the broadcasting team cringing for fear of a large FCC violation.

"Andi! Andrea! Are you okay?" I shout. I can't see her over the crowd of people. The other official is between us. I crane my neck and finally get a glimpse of her. Her eyes meet mine. She looks shaken.

Mike Barnaby's in my face waving a red card.

Sure, this he sees.

I nod and walk off without putting up a fight. I deserve this one. It was worth it.

As long as Andi's okay, anything's worth it.

CHAPTER 36: ANDI

I see the players as they barrel toward me. I attempt to sidestep them, but I don't get far enough over and Seamus O'Marra plows right into me. I curl forward as I fall so I don't whack my head again.

I don't need a second concussion this summer.

It still hurts when I make contact with the ground, especially with the weight of Seamus O'Marra on top of me. It's only for an instant as he jumps up as if I were made of fire. He grabs my wrists, pulling me to my feet.

While touching referees is a foul-able offense, this would be one time when it's okay.

What is not okay is when his hand snakes around my waist, cupping my butt and giving it a squeeze. It can't be misconstrued for the slap players give each other on the rear for encouragement.

Even so, I probably would have let that slide.

It's the wink and the grin he gives me that stuns me.

Is Mike going to call this? I reach my right hand around to my back pocket which is the signal that there is a red-card offense, but Mike just stares at me, unmoving. There's no way he didn't see it. Then, all hell breaks loose.

Out of nowhere, Brandon flies through the air, landing on Seamus and knocking him to the ground. Brandon's pommeling him as if he were in a bar fight. In a flash, Pressley Samson and TJ Doyle are pulling him off of Seamus.

Hamilton steps between the melee and me. "You okay?"

I nod, trying to look around him to see what's happening with Brandon. I hear my name before I can see him. "Andi! Andrea! Are you okay?"

He said *Andrea*.

I look around Hamilton Regan to see Mike giving Brandon a red card. He records the information before signaling a direct free kick for the Wave.

What about the red card for Seamus O'Marra?

I run up to Mike. "You've got to give O'Marra a card." We both glance at O'Marra who's still sitting on the ground, blood pouring from his obviously broken nose as the trainer attends to him.

Good. He deserves it.

"They're going to have to sub him out. He might have a concussion."

"He can get evaluated in the locker room when he's sent off. Did you not see my signal for a red?"

Mike sighs. "Andi, you can't give him a foul because he ran into you. You should have moved out of the way."

I grit my teeth. "I know I should have moved out of the way, but he shouldn't have touched my ass. GIVE HIM A RED CARD," I all but growl.

Mike rolls his eyes. "Fine, but you can't go carrying on every time something like this happens. If you want to be in the men's league, you have to toughen up a little. You know, not wear your heart on your sleeve so much." He turns away, holding up his red card again.

The crowd erupts into cheers.

It takes me a minute before I realize what they're chanting. "Andi! Andi! Andi!"

My breath rushes out. I scan the crowd, making eye contact with Hannah LaRosa in the first row. She's screaming my name at the top of her lungs. I smile and wave to the crowd, garnering even more applause.

Mike looks at me, exasperated. "Can we please finish this stupid game?"

I manage to stuff my feelings down for the last three minutes of play, plus nine minutes of stoppage time, much of which is thanks to Brandon Nix.

Brandon.

Oh, this is not going to be good for his career. He'd had such a good game. No fouls, a hat trick. And then he threw it all away.

For nothing.

Finally, Mike blows his whistle to signify the end of the game. I keep my head high as I exit the field and walk through the tunnel. There are too many eyes on me to let my emotions show. Once I finally make my way back to the referee locker room, I all but collapse, sagging against the wooden bench in front of my cubby. Mike comes in a moment later, totally hot.

"What the hell was that crap, Andi?"

I'm about to give Mike a comeuppance when Rico Lopez stands up. "We should be asking you the same question. What the hell was that crap, Mike? The touching was inappropriate. It's undeniable. Andi was signaling for a red card before the fight."

"Yeah, " Hamilton Regan joins in. "It's sad when Brandon Nix is the one who has your back rather than your colleagues."

Mike stares at me, seething.

That does it for me. I stand up too. "I was assaulted mid-game, Mike."

"He crashed into you. It was an accident."

"Are you blind?" Maybe the harassment referees get is not all totally unfounded. Maybe Mike needs to have his vision checked. "He grabbed my ass! It was no accident. It was on purpose, and it was inappropriate. He should be sanctioned or suspended or otherwise punished."

Mike tilts his head and gives me a tight smile. "I don't know that you're one to be making a big deal about inappropriate contact. I mean we all saw how Brandon Nix reacted. There has to be a reason for his behavior."

"What are you saying?"

"We've all heard the rumors. We've seen the videos."

I open my mouth and then close it again, not knowing what to say. I sit back down in silence. I can't explain his behavior without disclosing that we've spent time together.

In all fairness, until the event this morning I hadn't seen him in a month. One little kiss shouldn't change anything.

But it did.

Hamilton laughs. "Brandon Nix is a bad seed. He's a loose cannon, and there's no place in this league for someone that unhinged. We should make sure to request a drug screen, just to make sure he's not on something." He glances at me and continues, "But at least he did something."

I want to laugh because I know just how absurd that is. I need to stand up for Brandon like he did for me. But if I do, that's it. This will all be over. I need to think this through before I say or do anything incriminating.

There's got to be a way to save Brandon without sacrificing myself.

I'm tempted to storm out, still in my official kit. It's already going to be hard enough to get out to my car unbothered. Wearing my fluorescent yellow jersey will probably not aid and abet me.

Maybe if I move slowly enough, people will forget I exist. I take a long shower and am deliberate in packing up my gear. By the time I'm done, Mike's gone. Hamilton is still there.

"Walk you to your car?" he offers.

I nod, grateful for his courtesy and concern. I pull my phone out of my bag but hesitate to turn it on.

I can only imagine what's being said out there. I can only imagine the messages from the USSLRA, demanding my presence in Atlanta tomorrow at 8 a.m. sharp. I'm sure Benj will be checking on me to see if I'm okay.

Probably my mom and dad too, though they pretty much figure I can hold my own no matter what.

Hamilton and I walk side by side out to the parking lot. There are still people with their phones held up, trying to get pictures and videos. I ignore the calls of my name, certain that if I make eye contact or speak, I'll burst into tears.

Enough of me has been exposed today. I don't need the world to see that too.

Hamilton opens the driver's side door for me, and I slide in. "You good?" he asks as I turn the keys over and over in my hand without inserting them into the ignition.

I nod and he closes the door. I know he's not going to move until he sees me drive off. I put the car in drive, not thinking about where I'm going. I'm on autopilot as I head toward I-95. I see the sign for the exit and carefully glide over three lanes of traffic.

I should not be doing this.

This is stupid.

But at the end of the day—and what a day today was—this is the only place I want to be. I need to check and make sure he's okay. I need to thank him for coming to my defense.

KATHRYN R. BIEL

I can only imagine the fine the USSL is going to slap on him for this one.

But most of all, I just want to give him a hug.

I pull into his driveway and wait for Brandon to come home.

CHAPTER 37: BRANDON

My hand fucking hurts. So worth it.

I'm covered in sweat and dirt and blood, sitting here across from Bjorn Janssen and Bob Miller, the contents of my locker already packed in a bag at my feet. My soccer career ends today.

My agent is on speakerphone because he doesn't exert himself by doing things like coming to my games.

I'm not embarrassed about what I did. I am, however, mortified that Coach and Mr. Miller have to listen to the tirade coming from my dad's mouth.

"What the fuck were you thinking? You're a useless moron. I'm surprised you have enough brain cells to tie your own shoes. You—"

Mr. Miller reaches forward and pushes a button, ending the call. "I think this will be much more productive without his 'help.'" He holds up two fingers to quote that last word. I nod, saying nothing else.

The expression on Coach's face has shifted from disappointment to pity. I don't need his pity. Just cut me from the team and let me move on with my life.

It's time to rip the Band-Aid off. "What do you need me to sign? I'm sure I violated my code of conduct. I certainly violated the terms of my probation. I accept my termination. I'm not going to fight it."

Coach gives me a wan smile. "Did Brandon Nix just say he wasn't going to fight it?"

I return his expression. "I fight when things are worth fighting for. This isn't."

"Your career isn't worth fighting for? After playing a game like that? I wish you could see your growth over the past month, both on and off the field." Coach holds up his hands and offers one last statement. "Brandon, you're incredibly talented."

I look down at my hands. "I can be talented but that doesn't mean I didn't break the rules."

Coach looks at Mr. Miller, and for the first time, I sense a bit of desperation coming from him. "Is there anything we can do?"

Mr. Miller raises a hand to his chin, his gaze off in the distance, as he tries to solve a problem to which there is no solution.

I stand up, grabbing my duffle. "Look, I really do appreciate all you've done for me. Coach, I don't say this lightly when I say you've been more of a father to me than my own."

Bob Miller lets out a harsh laugh. "That's not saying much."

I keep talking. "You could continue my probation. You could suspend me for the rest of the season. You could fine me. But know this, at the end of the day, given the same circumstance, I would 100 percent do what I did today every single time. There is nothing you can do on your end to change that."

I turn and head for the door. As I'm about to cross the threshold, I hear Mr. Miller say, "Brandon?"

I look back at him.

"You need a new agent."

I nod and walk out of the Boston Buzzards facilities for the last time.

On the drive home, my confidence begins to wane. Not for what I said or did, because I stand by my statements. But for what a future without soccer means for me. I don't have a great grasp on what my finances are like. Everything goes through my dad.

He's not going to be pleased with me.

I'd say that it's okay; that I'm used to no one liking me. However, right now, I feel the furthest from okay that you can get. It feels like I've been torn open and am lying on the ground in a bloody heap.

I feel utterly alone.

Until I pull in my driveway and see the faded black Escape sitting there.

What's she doing here?

This is the last place she should be.

I slide my Porsche into the garage, anxiously putting it in park and exiting the vehicle. I grab my duffle out of the trunk, more from muscle memory than because I'll ever need it again. Andi's sitting on the bench next to my front door. "Why are you here?" I ask.

"Hello to you too," she says, standing up

I stop in front of her, dropping my bag on the ground. I don't know what to say. We stand there, staring at each other. Her hair is still pulled back like it was at the game, but it looks as if she's showered. Flyaways spring out around her face since she doesn't have the headband on to tame them any longer. She's wearing her warm-up shorts and jacket. She obviously came right from the stadium.

"You called me Andrea," she says finally.

"It's your name, isn't it?"

I see her eyes move up and down as they take in my appearance. "I still have to shower."

"I can smell that," Andi says matter-of-factly.

My mouth breaks into a wide grin. "Wanna help me?"

She tilts her head, matching my smile. "I don't suppose things can get worse than they currently are unless you're terrible in bed."

That makes me laugh. "I've never had any complaints before."

"You've probably never stuck around long enough to hear the complaints," she chides.

I take a step closer, pushing a loose hair off her face. "You'll have to let me know in the morning, Andrea."

That's all it takes. Her mouth is on mine, eager and hot. She tastes like heaven. Her arms encircle my neck. I slide my hand around her waist and then lower. I pull back slightly. "Is this okay?"

"You're the only one who has permission to touch my ass." She kisses me again.

I smile into her mouth. "And don't forget I'll pommel anyone who doesn't respect that."

Andi laughs, resting her forehead on my shoulder as she does. "I can't believe you did that."

"I can't believe he grabbed you."

She shrugs. "I wish I could say it was the first time. It probably won't even be the last. But if I want to run with the big dogs, I've got to be prepared to fetch the big stick."

I pull back. "Is that how the saying goes? I've never heard that one before."

Andi grabs my face with her hands and brings it close to hers. "I just made that up. But can we be done talking? I need to get you in the shower."

I can be done talking.

CHAPTER 38: ANDI

After several hours of ecstasy, I finally decide to bite the bullet and check my phone. As feared, the notifications are out of control. It's going to take me hours to go through all of these.

Brandon snores quietly next to me, his dark hair spilling on the pillow. I push it out of his face so I can see him more clearly. He looks younger without the stress of life on him.

I wish it could always be like this. But the weight of the phone in my hand reminds me that it's not. Careful not to wake him, I slide out of bed. His robe hangs on the back of the bathroom door, so I help myself to it.

My hair has been thoroughly destroyed. I look in the bathroom mirror. This is definitely the definition of bedhead. Lucky for me, Brandon has a cache of hair products and tools.

I've never been with a guy who had this kind of stuff. As I pull out my rubber band, it snaps. Brandon also has hair ties. Not gonna lie, the one he gave me the first time I was here has quickly become one of my favorites. I snag another one and twist it around my hair, now secured in a messy bun on the top of my head.

I creep downstairs and see a coffee pot on the counter. I fill it with grounds and water and set it to brew. Then, I grab a pad of paper from my bag and start taking notes, making a prioritized list of whom I have to contact.

Benj not only texted multiple times but he called too. He very rarely calls, so I know he was worried. He's my first response.

> *Me: I'm ok. I have a lot to work through, but I'm fine. I'll call you as soon as I can. Don't worry.*

He immediately texts back.

> *Benj: It's not every day my sister is assaulted on the job on national TV. I'm glad Nix pounded the shit out of him.*

Benj doesn't usually advocate for violence, so this is a surprise. So is his next text.

> *Benj: Still hate him? <winky emoji>*

The next set of messages are enough to wipe the smile from my face though. Though not unexpected, I was hoping that the outrageousness of Seamus O'Marra's conduct toward me would be enough to outweigh the implications of Brandon's reaction.

It does not appear as if luck was on my side with this one. As I read it, my stomach falls to the floor, and I'm overcome with the most intense desire to vomit. My mouth is dry, and my hands shake. I'm simultaneously cold yet sweating at the same time.

Dear Ms. Nichols,

Please be advised that I have scheduled a meeting with Samuel Fredericks on Tuesday, September 3 in the Atlanta main office to discuss the events of the game between the Miami Wave and the Boston Buzzards on September 1. You may bring your union representative with you.

Nathan Forget

No regards. No fondest wishes. No have a safe trip down here.

Simply come in tomorrow and meet with the president of the USSLRA. And bring a union rep.

That's probably what's got me the most scared.

I immediately forward this email to my union people and request someone to attend the meeting with me. I'm not sure how it works, but I hope for my sake whoever they send is good.

I write down on my list: *book flight to Atl*.

There are multiple requests from news organizations requesting a story or a comment. Those go in the ignore pile for right now.

Hannah texted me.

Hannah: Girl, you okay?

Short, sweet, and to the point.

I like Hannah LaRosa. I also know, from digging around her social media, that she helped Ophelia Henry find the information to exonerate Xavier Henry from whatever bad press he'd received that got him bounced from the British Football League. I should put her on a retainer to help Brandon.

Brandon.

I look around his oak-filled kitchen and put my head in my hands. What was I thinking? Coming here was probably the exact wrong thing to do. Kissing him was bad enough. Now, by sleeping with him, I've all but said goodbye to my career.

I deserve to be fired.

"Hey, whatcha doing?" Brandon stumbles into the kitchen. He's moving stiffly, almost limping. His right hand is raw and red.

I nod toward his hand. "You should've iced that last night."

"I should have iced my whole body, but I had better things to do." He leans down and kisses me lightly on the lips. "So what is it? Or is it top secret? More of your spy work?"

"Nothing classified here." I hold up my phone in one hand and the paper in the other. "Going through my phone. It blew up while I had it turned off."

Brandon pours himself a cup of coffee and sits down. "Anything good?"

"Well, my brother is, quote, *happy you beat the shit out of him*, end quote." That earns me a smile.

Brandon raises his eyebrows. "Anything else? Your face says there might be more than texts from Benj."

My heart does a double beat with the fact that Brandon remembered my brother's name.

"I have to fly to Atlanta for a meeting with HQ."

"That sounds ominous."

I nod. "Especially since it's not only with my manager, Nathan Forget, but the president of the USSLRA, Samuel Fredericks. They told me to bring my union rep."

"Shit."

"I know." I hold my mug of coffee cupped between both hands.

"What are you going to do?"

I stare at the brown liquid in my cup, hoping it has the answers like tea leaves are supposed to.

It does not.

"I don't know. I mean, best case, I'll never ref in the MUSSL again. My dream career is done."

Brandon cocks his head. "Why do you say that?"

I look around his kitchen then down at myself in his bathrobe. "I'd definitely say this counts as fraternizing. It's a fireable offense."

"Probably only with an active player. Which I'm not. I no longer play in the MUSSL. I'm not a soccer player anymore."

His words are like a punch to the gut. I reach out and put my hand on his. "Don't say that. Pay your fine. Serve your suspension. Do whatever they want you to do. Don't give up playing."

A pained expression crosses his face. "I already did. There wasn't much option, was there?"

"Well, you didn't have to pound Seamus O'Marra into the ground, though I'm glad you did."

"I did have to. No one touches you like that and gets away with it."

I'm trying to figure out where his passion for this is coming from. Hell, I could barely get Mike to call a foul on the guy. "Why? Why did you risk it all for me?"

Before he can answer that, my phone dings with another notification. It's James York, the union rep who will be attending the meeting. He asks me to call him.

"I'm sorry, Brandon, I have to make a call."

He stands up slowly, the toll of the game evident on his body. "No worries, I'm gonna go have a soak in my tub. Just don't fall off my treadmill while I'm in there."

"I didn't fall off the treadmill until you came back," I grumble.

Even though we're going to be speaking on the phone, not Face Timing, I don't feel right doing it sitting in Brandon's bathrobe with nothing else underneath. I run up to Brandon's room and throw on my clothes from yesterday. I feel gross, but this is the price you pay for booty calling without proper preparation.

I stop, midway through putting my shirt on. Booty call? Is that what this is? It certainly doesn't feel like a booty call. It doesn't feel like a one-night stand or a casual hookup.

I don't know what it feels like, but I don't think I've ever felt it before. It's *more*. It's pillow talk and breakfasts and watching seasons change. It's cooking in the same kitchen and picking each other up from the airport. It's calling from the car when it's been a bad day. It's falling into his arms every night.

It feels like it's worth sacrificing my career for.

I know that's a stupid, rash thing to think. It's a very Brandon-type of statement. But for once in my life, I'm not worrying about what would be easiest and most convenient for everyone else around me. As much as I want to keep refereeing, it is a finite career, based on my physical ability to keep up. I won't have that forever. For the first time, I'm looking beyond that to what I want to come home to every night.

Who I want to come home to every night.

The answer is undeniably clear.

As sure as I was that Brandon deserved a foul for kicking Trevyon Wallis-Smalls, I'm sure that we deserve *more* with each other.

I dial the number sent to me and discuss everything with James that's been said to me up to this point. He asks for emails and screenshots of what I have.

I wish I had a screen recording of that Zoom call where I asked about the salary charts.

I've already put everything on the line. If I'm going down, I'll make it in a blaze of glory.

"James ... there's this one other thing."

CHAPTER 39: BRANDON

Disappointed.

There's no other way to put it. I'm disappointed that Andi's fully dressed and practically out the door. I understand it, but that doesn't mean I have to like it. She has to go. She's got to get her shit organized before she flies to Atlanta.

I don't want her to leave.

Ever.

"Want me to go with you?" I ask, only half kidding. I don't want her to walk away. I want to spend hours—days—exploring her body and what this thing is between us.

I have never felt a pull like this before. It's like my whole world is off its axis, and she's the only thing propping me up.

The thought of her leaving makes it hard for me to breathe.

"I appreciate the offer, but I think you've helped enough this week," she says wryly.

I'm wearing the robe she just discarded. I could get dressed, but I'd rather be enveloped in her lavender-citrus scent for a while longer. I lounge on my side, my head propped on my hand. I stay on my bed, willing myself not to get up and drag her back here with me.

Andi's about to walk down the stairs when she stops. "We got sidetracked before. Why?"

"Why what?" I try to remember what we were talking about and when we got distracted.

"Why did you risk it all for me?"

I smile. "That's easy. Because you're worth it."

Andi closes her eyes and inhales for a moment. Then she's gone. I hear her footsteps run down the stairs. Then I hear the door open and shut. Her car turns over and backs out of the gravel driveway.

She's gone.

I roll flat, staring at my ceiling.

She'll come back.

She has to.

In the meantime, I contemplate never getting dressed and eating everything in my kitchen until I look like Thor, post-Thanos's snap.

I picture Andi, sitting at my kitchen table with her list of things to do to try and save her career. She just got up and did things. She made things happen.

She's like a machine.

Thinking about my multiple sessions with Watson Ross—damn, I'm probably going to have to find myself a new therapist—I evaluate Andi's actions.

From where I'm sitting—er, lying—it's easy to see that this is her trauma response. She shuts down and then attempts to control everything by micromanaging. I'm the opposite. I yell and scream and pretend nothing matters.

But now, something matters.

Andi matters.

I matter too.

With this new-found revelation, I decide to skip my self-destructive wallow-fest and do something. I get up and head downstairs. I dig through a drawer to find some scrap of paper. Seriously, does Andi carry paper on her at all times? Weird.

I start my list.

1. Fire Dad
2. Figure out what I want to be when I grow up

Okay, there's not much to go on, but it's a start at least.

I've got to be smart about number one. I scour my emails, trying to find all the accounts that my dad has started over the years in my name. Not an easy feat when you have over 10,000 emails, but the search bar is key.

Also, my dad may be the world's biggest asshole, but he's organized if nothing else. He likes making money, and he likes putting all those numbers in spreadsheets to add them up.

He also uses a financial advisor to manage all my accounts.

Bingo.

I've never signed a legal contract with my father to act as my agent. It just was, and no one questioned it. I signed whatever I needed to whenever I needed to. I log in to each and every account, double-checking.

His name is not on a single one.

He didn't give me enough credit to ever want to take control of this. Maybe he didn't think I was smart enough. Doesn't matter. I must be the luckiest son of a bitch alive. First Andi and then this.

Now it's time to change my passwords.

It takes me all day and several calls, but I've done it. I've talked with the financial advisor who is now aware that Nicholas Nix will no longer be acting on my behalf. Based on the shape my accounts are in, I'd say my financial advisor is doing a bang-up job, so I keep everything where it is.

Now it's time for the hardest phone call of all.

"Hey, Dad."

There's silence on the line. He's still there, just giving me the silent treatment.

"So, I'm not playing with the Boston Buzzards anymore."

"You're going to be a hard sell anywhere at this point. No one wants someone like you."

Andi wants me.

"Well, I guess it's good for me that I don't want to play soccer right now."

"You're just saying that. In two days you'll be regretting it. I'll have to act quickly, but maybe the Baltimore Terrors are sketchy enough to take you on amidst all the controversy."

No doubt about it, I'm going to have to find another therapist ASAP. There's so much here to unpack.

"I told you, I'm done playing soccer."

"What do you think you're going to do? You have no other skills. And it's not like you have endorsements to fall back on."

Suddenly my lack of endorsement deals seems totally clear. I thought my dad wanted to keep as much money for himself as he could. In reality, he thought it was an ace up his sleeve. One he'd play—like he is right now—when he needed to control me.

"I dunno what I'm going to do. Maybe I'll go play football. I've always wanted to do that. I'll figure it out. All I know is I'll be doing it without you. You're officially fired as my agent. I've sent you an email with the details of your termination. Have a nice life, Dad. I certainly plan to."

I disconnect and then promptly block him.

It feels amazing.

I shoot Andi a text message.

Me: *Thinking about you. Hope everything is going well for you. I've got amazing news on my end, if you want to hear it. If not, no worries.*

She promptly texts back.

Andi: Of course I want to hear your news, but I'm just about to take off for Atlanta. I need to do a bunch of research for my meeting and pre-game with James. Don't take this the wrong way, but you're a distraction.

I smile at this.

Me: In a good way or a bad way?

Andi: In the best way. I'll call you when I have an update. I can't wait to hear your news.

I'm tempted to keep texting, but she said in black and white that she has work to do. I can respect that.

Without anything else to distract me, I replay the conversation with my father in my head. He's right. I have nothing to do. Except one thought bounces around my brain, refusing to stop. Refusing to quiet. Refusing to let me think of anything else.

It's a stupid idea.

It really is.

Not to mention, it'll never work.

That may all be true, but I'm still me. I'm still going to go for it. It worked with Andi. Maybe there's a chance with this too?

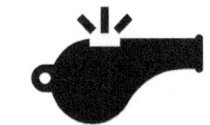

CHAPTER 40: ANDI

I pull at my skirt, wishing it was longer and less fitted in the thighs. I'm more muscular than I have been in years, which means I feel like a stuffed sausage in this pencil skirt that I bought for job interviews when I got out of PT school.

I'm a little unsteady on my black pumps, not used to such a narrow, unstable shoe.

I don't know what one is supposed to wear for a disciplinary hearing, but I imagine it's like this. I feel like I'm playing dress-up.

No matter how many times I write out my statement of the events since the beginning of July with my first head refereeing game, I can see the truth in my words. I might as well put a heart-eyes emoji every time I write Brandon's name and dot the "i" in Nix with an oversized heart. That's how obvious it is.

Life was much easier when I was invisible. When I didn't take up space and when no one saw me. I could pass neatly through, unnoticed.

This is messy.

I flip the page in my yellow legal pad. This is the page of the number calculations. This is why I have to be messy.

I want justice.

I know life isn't fair. I know it all too well. If life were fair, Benj wouldn't have SMA. I wouldn't have had to grow up feeling that I couldn't voice discontent about anything because it didn't compare to what my brother was going through. I wouldn't be so worried about my parents' stress that I never let them see my needs.

This isn't about that kind of fairness.

This is about gender equality.

I don't know how long the USSLRA thought they could get away with it. I'm guessing for a while. Maybe it's why they've been so slow to hire women, even when their professional counterpart, the British Football League, has been diversifying for years.

James York is waiting for me in the parking lot of the USSLRA headquarters. I come here at least three times a year for performance reviews, fitness tests, and professional development. This place has always filled me with excitement.

Until today.

What if I lose it all?

"How are you doing?" James asks.

"I feel like I'm going to puke."

He nods. "Keep it brief. You do have to answer their questions, but don't overtalk."

I raise an eyebrow.

He laughs. "Right. I don't even have to tell you this. You're known for holding it all close to the vest anyway. I'm sure that's one reason why they thought the salary gap wouldn't be an issue. You're not one to raise a fuss."

His words feel like a slap in the face. Unintentional, sure, but they hurt nonetheless. He's basically saying I'm being punished for not taking up more space; for not screaming and yelling and pitching a fit. Of course, we all know if I did those things, I'd be labeled as a hysterical female.

There's no winning, is there?

If keeping silent lets them take advantage of me, then maybe it's time for me to get loud.

Maybe Brandon has been on to something after all.

WWBND?

I don't think anyone in the history of Forever has asked "What Would Brandon Nix Do?" but I'm also not sure anyone else knows him like I do. He's so much more than he seems at first glance.

Sure, some of it is a little caveman for me, but he wasn't the one accosting me during a game. He was the one caring for me. He was the one who risked everything to protect me.

Suddenly, I know what I need to do.

I flip to the third page of my notepad and signal James that I'm ready to go.

I walk through the lobby with my head held high, bolstered by confidence in my decision. If I go down, I'm going down swinging, just like Brandon did.

Figuratively, not literally, like he did. But still.

Waiting for me in the conference room is not only Nathan Forget and Samuel Fredricks, but also an attorney. Interesting.

I smile and wait for my moment.

"Thank you, Andi, for coming down today," Nathan begins. "I'm sure you've been able to surmise that we'd like to speak to you about the conduct that occurred at the Miami Wave–Boston Buzzards game this past weekend."

I nod. It's the perfect introduction. "Yes, thank you. I was going to ask for a meeting had you not reached out first. According to"—I glance down at my notes—"*Commonwealth v. Vasquez* and *Commonwealth v. Mosby*, quoting *Commonwealth v. De La Cruz*, the state of Massachusetts, where the game in question took place, defines a touching as 'an incident when, judged by the normative standard of societal mores, it is violative of social and behavioral expectations in a manner which is fundamentally offensive to contemporary moral values and which the common sense of society would regard as immodest, immoral, and improper. It has been held that the intentional, unjustified touching of private areas such as the breasts, abdomen, buttocks, thighs, and pubic area of a female constitutes an indecent assault and battery.' I assume this was the conduct you wanted to address?"

The silence in the room is deafening.

I wait, willing the sweat not to bead up at the edge of my forehead and trickle down, showing my hand.

Samuel Fredericks clears his throat. "Um, yes, well, we'll have to look into it."

"While you're looking at the video of the assault I suffered while working in your employment during the execution of my job, would you also please take a closer look at the Equal Pay Act of 1963? It requires that men and women in the same workplace be given equal pay for equal work. According to my calculations, the wages I receive for officiating MUSSL and WUSSL games are approximately 18 percent less than that of a male counterpart who is working at the same level as me."

I hold Samuel Frederick's gaze until he looks away. The red tinge to the rim of his ears gives it all away.

"Was there anything else you wanted to discuss, or were those two points enough?" I sit back and demurely fold my hands on top of my legal pad.

The nervous look shared between the three men is enough to make my heart race. I think I've won.

"We'd like to discuss Brandon Nix with you," the attorney begins. Here it comes. "And the possibility of the compromised impartiality it may have caused."

"I'm sure you have reviewed and scored my performance, just like you do for all officials for every match. What deductions did I receive that day? Were there any specific to Brandon Nix?"

Nathan shakes his head.

"Anything that could be construed as bias toward the Boston Buzzards or against the Miami Wave?"

Another head shake.

"Nathan, were there any missed calls on my part that you could see? Should I not have called Brandon Nix offside? He looked offside from my vantage point."

"He was offside," Nathan mumbles, his head down.

"Then what would you like me to explain?"

"Um, can you explain the reaction of Brandon Nix? Why did he attack Seamus O'Marra in such a violent way?"

"Normally, I'd reply with something like, 'can anyone explain what Brandon Nix does?' However, Mr. Nix and I had spent some time working together on a charity event. While there's never been any love lost between us, the event caused us to put our petty differences aside for the greater good. In our limited interactions, we have been cordial. I can only assume that Mr. Nix saw me being so egregiously violated that he felt the need to take matters into his own hands. I cannot condone that behavior, and I would expect a hefty penalty for him, just as I would expect the same, if not worse, for Mr. O'Marra. While there is precedence for violence in sports, there is not for sexual assault." I stand up. "Please let me know how you plan to address the pay issue, including retroactive pay for what I can only assume is a clerical error, as well as the punishment for Seamus O'Marra."

I stand up and walk out, leaving the room full of men behind.

If you want something done properly, ask a woman.

CHAPTER 41: BRANDON

Thank you for meeting with me today." I shake Justice Williams's hand. "I appreciate how quickly you were able to make this happen."

Justice sits down and smiles. "I'm going to have to start paying Callaghan Entay a commission for new clients. First Xavier Henry and now you."

I smile tightly. "I'm not sure you want me for a client. I'm not sure anyone does."

"Your reputation certainly precedes you, that's for sure. I like a good challenge though."

I fiddle with the glass of water in front of me. We're meeting for lunch at Davio's Italian Steakhouse outside Foxborough. I asked Callaghan if his agent would be willing to talk with me about a possible idea.

It's most likely a stupid idea, but that doesn't mean it won't work.

Justice waits patiently for me to start. I'm not normally ever at a loss for words. This time, I want to be careful about what I say. I don't want to blurt something out simply for shock value.

There's going to be enough shock if this plan can come to fruition.

"Full disclosure, up to this point, my agent-manager has always been my father. There was never a legally binding contract. However, I have officially terminated him. I'd like to go in a different direction."

"I would hope so. It didn't seem like you had much of a direction at all. You've had a lot of missed opportunities, and I don't just mean shots on goal."

I give Justice a tight smile. "That is the truth. I also had very little guidance, support, or career management. It mostly consisted of criticism and beratement after a public display of my outgoing personality."

Justice laughs. "Is that what we're calling it?"

I shrug. "For now. I'm working with a therapist, and that, along with … someone else … have helped me understand how my behavior may have been a stumbling block in my career."

"Someone else?" He raises his eyebrows

I'm not ready to even soft launch the possibility of Andi and me to the public, especially when I haven't heard from her today. Just because I gave my career up for her doesn't mean she owes me anything.

That's not true. I didn't give my career up for her. I wasn't in the right place, and the work I did on myself helped me realize that. Plus, what Seamus O'Marra did was 100 percent wrong, and I will never regret calling him on it the way I did.

"Okay, well, here's what I'm thinking." I slide the manilla folder across the table. Justice flips it open and scans the outline on the single piece of paper inside. He closes it and folds his hands on top.

His gaze is downright penetrating. I squirm in my seat. Finally, he clears his throat. "This is an interesting proposal."

"You can see why I need your help."

Justice pulls out his phone and scrolls through before holding the phone to his ear. "Hey Raul, it's Justice. You remember that thing we were talking about during golf last week? Yeah, well, I think I know how to make it happen. When are you free?" Justice maintains eye contact with me as he agrees to a meeting place and time before disconnecting.

"What's your schedule look like for the rest of the week?"

I laugh. "I'm pretty open."

"Good. Raul's in LA for some event, so we're heading out there." He doesn't look up as he says this, furiously typing in his phone. "My assistant, Heaven, will text you the itinerary as soon as she has it. We'll fly out tonight."

"This quickly?"

"It's the beginning of September, which means we only have seven months until the draft. Combine is in five. That's not a lot of time to line up everything we need to get in place. We're already behind schedule."

"So you'll take me as a client?" This is all happening so fast. My head is spinning.

Justice holds up the folder. "For this project only. If this project does not come to fruition, then we'll have to renegotiate. Where did this idea come from?"

I tap the side of my head. "Desperate times call for desperate measures."

"Do you think you can do it?"

I nod. "Physically, yes. Conduct-wise, pretty sure?" I'm going to be honest with him. "I'm not going to create drama for the sake of drama, but I am who I am. I don't have a great internal filter."

"That's what I'm counting on. This is gold, Brandon. Pure gold. And I'm so excited to see what we can do. Now let's get packed for LA."

As we stand to leave, Justice asks, "Why? Why this?"

"It's what I've always wanted, in reality."

"It's a huge risk."

I nod. "I know it is. But if I stayed where I was, it would cost someone else what they've always dreamed of. I can't do that to her. If this works, we both get what we've always wanted."

"And you get her?"

"That's the plan."

CHAPTER 42: ANDI

After the most exhausting three days of my life, I'm finally back in Boston. I take the T back to my place where I promptly re-pack my bag and get in my car.

I feel like I'm in the movie *Planes, Trains, and Automobiles*.

I cannot wait to see Brandon; to tell him everything that happened. James York didn't want me saying anything until the official statements were released, not even to Brandon.

It's been hard.

Never before, even when I was with Mike, have I ever had a desire to share with someone like this. I'm not made of glass when I'm around Brandon. That knowledge gave me the strength to stand up and be seen at the USSLRA headquarters.

Things are changing because of me.

The threat of a massive class action lawsuit alone was enough to get them to draw up a contract with all female referees, ensuring not only equal pay scales, but guaranteeing retroactive pay for the 18 percent differential. They are also increasing the rate for the WUSSL games to equal those of the MUSSL games. Moving forward, there will be one pay scale for all games, regardless of the gender of either the officials or the players. The ink's not quite dry—because bureaucracy—but if they don't come through, there'll be hell to pay.

Additionally, the implementation of the video assistant referee next season will not only create 25 percent more jobs, but it will also be a viable option for women who are pregnant or postpartum to continue working and not lose progress on their way to promotion.

My name has officially been cleared of any wrongdoing regarding the Seamus O'Malley–Brandon Nix fight. Both players will receive hefty fines and a two-game suspension. There is no call for Brandon to be expelled from the league.

He can keep playing.

I've disclosed my relationship with Brandon. If he continues playing, I'll only be officiating games in the WUSSL.

He's worth that trade-off.

Because of the aforementioned deal, it won't be a pay cut for me, and I'll still get to advance my career. Then I can go to watch the Boston Buzzards play as a WAG. It really is the perfect outcome.

Perfect until I get to Brandon's place and it's empty.

That's disappointing.

In the few brief texts we'd exchanged over the past few days, he didn't mention traveling. Maybe he's at the grocery store?

My call goes directly to voicemail.

That's not a good sign.

Not that we've called each other that much, but he's never declined my call before. It's after 9 p.m., so the options of where he could be are limited.

I'm sure he'll be back soon.

I get back in my car to wait. And wait. And wait.

After about an hour, the panic starts to set in. Not the "I hope he wasn't in an accident" kind of panic, but the "what did I just do with my career" type.

I'd texted him I was coming back today and that I'd be down as soon as I could. My arrival here is not a surprise.

The only thing that's a surprise is how much of a fool I was. I can't believe I jumped in with my whole chest like this. I could easily have been fired when I disclosed that—post Wave–Buzzards game—I entered into a relationship with Brandon.

I'm sure they didn't believe me that nothing happened prior to that, but they weren't really in a position to fight me on anything.

But as I sit here in Brandon's driveway, looking at his dark house, I wonder why I did all this. None of it felt wrong. In fact, it all felt very right. I don't know how I could have missed the mark so completely and totally. I wish there was a video-assisted replay for this whole thing so I could see where I went wrong.

The tears start, hot and furious. I let them fall. I don't remember the last time I cried. It feels unnatural at first. I'm not used to letting my body respond this viscerally to my feelings. Now that those floodgates are open, I don't know if I'll ever be able to stem this tide.

My chest heaves as I gasp for breath. My body is shaking, convulsing almost. Snot is running out of my nose as wails escape my mouth. I—

Knock knock knock.

"Aah!" I scream, jumping at the movement and noise outside my car window.

I hear the deep rumbling laughter, but it does nothing to calm my heart which is about to pound its way through my chest wall.

"Andi, what are you doing?"

I swallow and swipe quickly at the tears on my cheeks. I glance in the rearview mirror and then wish instantly I hadn't. My eyes are red and swollen. I look terrible.

I'm pretty sure I looked better when I wiped out on the treadmill.

"I'm fine," I blurt.

"Obviously not," Brandon says as he opens the door. "What's going on?"

"You weren't here. I haven't talked to you in three days and you weren't here when I got back. I thought ... maybe ..." I don't finish. I don't know how to express what I'm feeling.

Fear?

Panic?

Loneliness?

"I just got in from Logan. I thought maybe I'd see you there."

"Logan? What were you doing there? Where did you go?" I continue wiping at my face with my hands and eventually give up and use the hem of my shirt.

"Are you going to get out of the car or are we going to stand here and talk in the driveway all night?"

I glance over my shoulder at the overnight bag in the back seat. Was I jumping the gun? Was I being presumptive?

When I turn back to face him, I see Brandon's gaze trained on the rear seat as well. He opens the back door and grabs the bag. "Okay, well, I'm getting eaten alive by mosquitos, so I'm going in. Join me when you're ready."

I watch him walk into the house, still trying to calm my breathing and figure out what the hell is going on with me. It's nice to see Brandon is as blunt as ever.

Actually, it was just what I needed. There was no pressure to stop reacting. To stop feeling. He didn't ask me to push everything down and put it neatly away. He implied he would be waiting for me when I was ready. It was on my timeline, not his.

I mean, he did take my bag, so I can't just leave, which means he does want me to stay.

He wants me.

I didn't do this huge thing, take a big risk for nothing. There is a prize for stepping outside my comfort zone and showing my feelings. And that prize is waiting inside for me.

It's time to go get my reward.

CHAPTER 43: BRANDON

What the hell is taking her so long?

I mean, she was a total mess. I've never seen her that uncontrolled. Not when she wiped out on the treadmill. Not as the crowd was booing her walking onto the field during her first game. Not as Seamus O'Marra was groping her in front of 20,000 fans plus a live televised audience.

Something must have gone terribly wrong in Atlanta.

Andi finally walks in with a sheepish grin on her face. I don't even let her speak. "We'll fight this. We'll sue. Don't worry about lawyers. I'll pay for them."

She tilts her head, creasing her eyebrows. "For what?"

"Did they fire you? We'll sue."

Andi shakes her head.

"Why were you hysterical in my driveway?"

"Because you weren't here."

"I was on my way to you. I was running late."

She laughs. "You know I hate it when people are late."

I hold up my hands. "This time, I swear it wasn't me. The entire flight was late. Blame the crosswinds. I know I'm full of hot air and all, but even I don't make enough to change the flight pattern."

"Where were you?"

"On a job interview. In California."

Andi nods, sinking down onto the couch. "Right. The Sacramento Saints." She blows out a long breath. "We'll figure something out. I mean, that is, if you want to. No pressure. This isn't really a thing. Forget I said anything. I should be going."

I cross the room in three steps and squat down in front of her, effectively blocking her from standing up. "You're not going anywhere. And neither am I. Not yet at least."

"What about the Sacramento Saints?"

"If I went to the Saints, what would that do to you?"

She looks down at her hands, tightly twisted together in her lap. "I'd miss you. Long distance is hard."

My heart catches. "What about your job? How would you ref a game if I was playing?"

She looks up at me. "I wouldn't. I'm not going to be reffing for the MUSSL anymore."

Shit, that's why she's so upset. She lost her job because of me and then thought I deserted her. "Andrew, you cannot give up your job for me."

"It's already done, so don't worry about it. And before you try to tell me differently, you're worth it. I'm not gonna say it's fine, because we all know it's never fine when I say that. It's good. They're adjusting the pay, so I won't be making less in the WUSSL. I also won't have to deal with assholes like O'Marra, so it's actually good. We both win."

I feel my face fall. How am I going to tell her?

Her expression matches my own. "Oh. Oh ... I see. I ..." She stands up, pushing me out of the way, practically climbing over me. "I didn't mean to assume that we would be together. But I had to be upfront with them. There was a lot on the line for a lot of people, and I didn't want to jeopardize it all by hiding us."

"Andi, you didn't need to do that."

She swallows, looking around. She spies her bag in the corner and moves across the room to pick it up. "I'm sorry that I dragged you into this. Don't worry about me. It'll be better this way. You won't have to see me at your games."

She won't let me get a word in edgewise. "Andrea, stop!" I yell, if only to get her to cease talking. "Would you let me speak?"

Her mouth snaps shut, her eyes growing wide. I'd better take my opportunity while it's here.

"I wasn't out talking to the Sacramento Saints. You didn't need to sacrifice your role in the MUSSL because I'm done playing soccer." I hold my hand up to her lips. "And before you tell me I shouldn't have done that, yes, I should have. Soccer isn't my passion. It never has been. And if the choice came down to you having the job of your dreams or me being in a job that I'm ambivalent about, then it was an easy decision. Anyone can see that. Even if you don't want to be with me, you should be doing the thing you love."

"I want to be with you," she breathes.

That's all I need to hear.

"Good. I want to be with you. We are together. It's official. So as long as we're done jumping to conclusions, can we jump into bed?"

Andi laughs. "You really are a Neanderthal, aren't you?"

I pick her up, slinging her over my shoulder. "Let me show you the ways."

Andi pulls her hair up into a ponytail, using my favorite red hair tie. "I'm never getting that back, am I?"

"Some girls steal hoodies. I steal hair ties."

"Is this a thing you do?"

Andi laughs. "I've never been with anyone with long hair before. If you'd have asked me a few weeks ago, I'd have said the man bun was a deal breaker."

"And now?" I'm propped on my elbow, our bodies flush. My hair is a mess, and in all honesty, I could use a hair tie too.

"Almost everything I thought about you was wrong, Brandon Nix."

She's piqued my curiosity. "What did you think about me?"

"I thought I hated you as much as I hate raisins masquerading as chocolate chips in cookies."

I put my hand over my chest, feigning shock. "You hated me? Do you still hate me?"

She lifts her head off the pillow, her lips meeting mine. "I definitely don't hate you."

"I don't hate you either."

"Since we agree on that, are you ever going to tell me what you're working on for a job, or are you just going to keep distracting me with your sexy body?"

"Is that what I'm doing?" I trail a line of kisses along the length of her collarbone. "I'd say you're distracting me."

"Brandon, just tell me!" she shrieks.

I squint at her, trying to figure out how to best deliver the news. "It's not 100 percent finalized yet, but my agent—"

"Your dad?"

"No, I fired him. My new agent, Justice Williams, is working to get me a reality TV show deal, so it's a good thing you told the USSLRA about us. Otherwise, they'd find out when they turn on the TV this spring."

"What if I don't want to be on TV?" She looks a little pale.

"You can be on as much or as little as you want."

Andi props herself up on her elbows, forcing me to back up. I don't like having to put space between us. I'm not sure I ever will. "What are you doing that necessitates a TV show?"

"Necessitates is a strong word." I'm purposely being evasive because I can see how she's chomping at the bit to know.

"What is the TV show about?"

"Me."

"What about you?"

"You know, this and that. What I'm up to on a daily basis. That sort of thing."

"Brandon ..."

"Andrew ..." I match her tone and expression. Except I can't hold her stony look anymore and I start laughing. "I'm going to attempt to make history by being the first professional soccer player to also start in the National Football League as a placekicker. The show is going to follow my journey as I train and then do the combine and hopefully get a job."

Andi sits up. "You're going to be a football player?"

"I'm trading in my football cleats for football cleats."

"Why?"

This is easy. "Because this way, I can do what I've always wanted to do instead of what my parents wanted for me. You can do what you've always wanted to do instead of what your parents wanted for you."

Her eyes grow wide as her mouth falls open. I've rendered her speechless. For once. Time to put that ball right between the goalposts.

"And we can be together. This way, everyone wins."

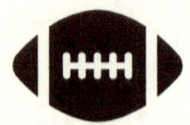

EPILOGUE: ANDI

I try to school my expression as I feel the camera zoom in. In the year since Brandon and I got together, I've lost my poker face. Mostly because I don't have to hide anymore. I don't have to be invisible anymore.

Right now, I'd like to be, though.

I don't need the entire world to see me freak out.

This past winter, he trained like nobody's business, gaining 15 pounds of pure muscle to get him to a more competitive weight by the February combine.

Even without the contracted television cameras, Brandon certainly amassed a lot of attention this year. With Hannah LaRosa's help, his ClikClak account has taken off. He has over two million followers now. It's more than just temporary social media fame. From the most cards in a professional soccer season to the oldest player ever drafted in the NFL (33 years and 2 days) to the only person to ever play at the top professional level for both soccer and football, Brandon's in the history books.

I am too, as the first female soccer referee to reach Level 2 status and be primarily stationed in the MUSSL.

All in all, it's been a stellar year for both of us.

I'm sitting at the 50-yard line of the New England Patriots and New York Jets game with Brandon's sister, Jess, and her boyfriend Jasper. Benj and Sam are here too.

Benj is now the president of the Brandon Nix fan club. At least that's what the shirt Brandon gave Benj for Christmas says.

Later that night, in the darkness of my childhood bedroom, he whispered that while Benj's shirt was hilarious, seeing me with his name on my shirt had other effects.

I enjoyed that Christmas gift tremendously.

But now is *definitely* not the time to be thinking about that.

Hannah's down on the sidelines, getting pictures and footage. Several of Brandon's former teammates from the Buzzards are here as well, but they're sitting somewhere else. I'm trying to keep as much distance from them as possible, though they're a pretty good group of guys.

It's the second possession of the game for the Patriots. If this drive is successful, the Patriots will score a touchdown, which should be a good thing. Except that means Brandon will make his debut as their placekicker to make the extra point. I see him on the sideline, warming up. He kicks into the net a few times as the quarterback throws the ball squarely into the end zone.

Oh shit, this is it.

I watch my man take the field. Soccer shorts may do wonders for a player's thighs, but football pants are simply magical on the backside.

At least Brandon's backside.

Brandon sprints out onto the field. He's run all the math with me a thousand times. The extra point is kicked from a distance of roughly 33 yards. But then it has to be launched vertically as well. The crossbar is approximately 10 feet off the ground, but most players have a vertical jump of …

I stopped listening when he got into the physics behind the differences in the shapes of the soccer ball versus the football. It was amazing to see how happy this made him. The light in his eyes when he talks about playing football is something I'd never have predicted.

Just like I'd never have predicted how good he'd look with short hair. It was part of his image makeover for the show, and let me just say, I like it.

A lot.

I also like that I inherited Brandon's hair-tie collection.

The Pats get in formation. I put my hands over my eyes and then peek through my fingers. Brandon's out there, raising his arm up and down to line up where he needs to be. The ball is snapped. Brandon takes three steps back and then three steps forward swinging and kicking and ... he misses.

No good.

The fans boo.

I sit down, my face blank. Oh Brandon, he's got to be crushed. He runs off the field as the punter trots out to kick the ball away. The Jets receive it and begin running, only to fumble it. It's recovered by the Patriots and returned for a touchdown.

Just like that, it's Brandon's turn again.

I really can't watch this time. I put my head down and wait. The roar of the crowd tells me all I need to know.

He made it.

I jump to my feet, screaming and clapping. Jess grabs me, and we bounce up and down holding onto each other as if that one point just won the Superbowl. The look on his face as he takes his helmet off is one of pure joy.

An agonizing three hours later, the game is still going. I know people criticize soccer for being slow because there's not a lot of scoring, but American football takes forever.

Too many commercial breaks.

The Patriots ran away with the game. It's 37–7 with two minutes left on the clock. The math on that is Brandon made four out of five extra-point attempts and one field goal from 45 yards. For those who have him in their fantasy leagues, he scored seven points.

That's also important because one of his corporate sponsors is donating a thousand dollars for every point scored to JustSibs.

As the time ticks away on the fourth quarter, Jess and I make our way down to the front row. Benj and Sam can't weave their way down to the field the same way, but Hannah has given them passes to get on-field access. We'll meet them down there. We have family passes hung on lanyards around our necks, so we're allowed through without difficulty. Having a camera crew for the series finale of *American Football Hero* doesn't hurt our access.

This will be the last part they film, at least for now.

Having a production team attached to his training journey certainly helped Brandon get noticed. His performance, as evidenced by this game, secured him the spot.

Brandon looks up to the stands, searching. His gaze lands on me and his mouth breaks into a huge grin. I match his expression.

I love seeing his smile. I love seeing the joy that playing this sport brings him. I love him.

He waves at us and then motions for us to come closer. We get up to the rail, still about seven feet above Brandon's head.

"Come on over," he yells as the final whistle blows. There will be media down on the field, so it's not like they're in a mad dash for the locker room. At least the Patriots aren't. The Jets might be another story.

I swing one leg over the railing and then the other. Brandon's standing underneath me, his arms raised and ready to catch me.

"Just go for it. I've got you."

No other statement could better sum up our relationship.

I jump down and Brandon catches me, my body slamming into his. Certainly not graceful, and I'd bet there's at least one camera that's recorded it for posterity.

Brandon plants a quick kiss on my lips and then lets his hands drop. He stands inches from my face.

Love.

I love listening to the sound of water lap the banks of the lake. I love taking an ice bath followed by a hot shower to ease the pain in my aching body after a fulfilling, yet grueling workout. I love waking up to the most beautiful brown eyes every morning.

I love Brandon Nix.

"You did it," I yell over the volume in the stadium.

"We did it, Andrew."

I have to laugh. "Why with the Andrew still?"

"Because I love how riled up it gets you. Because I love how it makes your eyes sparkle. Because I love you."

Brandon takes a step back and then another and then another. Then, he's down on one knee, pulling a small ring box out from—hell I don't even know where he's had it.

"Andrea Nichols, will you—"

I don't even wait for him to finish. I rush him, tackling him to the ground, planting my lips firmly on his as I scream, "YES! YES! YES!" He rolls me over and somehow manages to slip the diamond ring on my finger. I look up to see not only Benj and Sam,

Jess and Jasper, but several of Brandon's new teammates surrounding us.

Not to mention multiple cameras.

Now that's a video I can't wait to see go viral.

THE END

ACKNOWLEDGMENTS

To Nathanaël de Wilde: Thank you for answering my questions about being a professional soccer referee and what goes into it. Emailing across a language barrier is never easy. Merci beaucoup.

To Katie Holcomb and Ryan's Case for Smiles/JustSibs/Coping Space: First of all, thank you for the work you do. Second, thank you for letting me share your organization in my book. I hope I did it justice.

To Dianna Koch: Thank you for explaining what your concussion felt like. I'm sorry your head got smashed in the first place, but since I know how the story ended, I know it's all good. By the way, you do have a kid in college.

To my beta readers, Liz O'Donnell and Tara Roberts. Thank you for giving me feedback on my baby.

To Michele: I'll never have enough words to thank you for being my person. But I'm not sorry at all I made you cry in Northway Toyota.

To Jessica Klein: Your work on the figures for the cover of this series is perfect.

To my editors, Tami Lund and Regina Dowling: Thank you, thank you, thank you for taking this book to the next level.

ABOUT THE AUTHOR

Armed with quick wit, relatable character, themes of resilience, and always a happy ending, award-winning and *USA Today* Bestselling author Kathryn R. Biel writes comfort reads. Balancing drama and angst with laughter and love, Kathryn weaves stories that will whisk you away for a few hours and have you rooting for the underdog, whether it's through sports romance, romantic comedy, or lighter women's fiction. By day, Kathryn is a pediatric physical therapist and Chief Domestic Officer of the Biel household. By night, when not writing, Kathryn can be found at the dance studio, knitting, watching sports with her husband and son, cuddling with her four cats, embarrassing herself on TikTok, and doing absolutely anything to avoid cleaning her house.

Kathryn is the author of 21 books, including the award-winning *Live for This*, *Made for Me*, and *The UnBRCAble Women Series (Ready for Whatever, Seize the Day,* and *Underneath It All)*.

Scan now to instantly receive FREE exclusive bonus content!

Stand Alone Books:

Good Intentions
Hold Her Down
I'm Still Here
Jump, Jive, and Wail
Killing Me Softly
Live for This
Once in a Lifetime
Paradise by the Dashboard Light

Boston Buzzards:
XOXO
You Belong with Me
Zero to Hero

A New Beginnings Series:
Completions and Connections: A New Beginnings Novella
Made for Me
New Attitude
Queen of Hearts

The UnBRCAble Women Series:
Ready for Whatever
Seize the Day
Underneath It All

Center Stage Love Stories:
Act One: *Take a Chance on Me*
Act Two: *Vision of Love*
Act Three: *Whatever It Takes*

If you've enjoyed this book, please help the author out by leaving a review on your favorite retailer and **Goodreads.** A few minutes of your time makes a huge difference!

www.ingramcontent.com/pod-product-compliance
Lightning Source LLC
Chambersburg PA
CBHW060428030726
47495CB00003B/789